GUNS OF THE RIMROCK

GUNS OF THE RIMROCK

D. B. Newton

GUNSMOKE

First published in the UK by Sampson Low

This hardback edition 2013
by AudioGO Ltd
by arrangement with
Golden West Literary Agency

ISBN 978 1 471 32135 1

British Library Cataloguing in Publication Data available.

Printed and bound in Great Britain by
MPG Books Group Limited

D(wight) B(ennett) Newton is the author of a number of notable Western novels. Born in Kansas City, Missouri, Newton went on to complete work for a Master's degree in history at the University of Missouri. From the time he first discovered Max Brand in Street and Smith's *Western Story Magazine,* he knew he wanted to be an author of Western fiction. He began contributing Western stories and novelettes to the Red Circle group of Western pulp magazines published by Newsstand in the late 1930s. During the Second World War, Newton served in the US Army Engineers and fell in love with the central Oregon region when stationed there. He would later become a permanent resident of that state and Oregon frequently serves as the locale for many of his finest novels. As a client of the August Lenniger Literary Agency, Newton found that every time he switched publishers he was given a different byline by his agent. This complicated his visibility. Yet in notable novels from *Range Boss* (1949), the first original novel ever published in a modern paperback edition, through his impressive list of titles for the Double D series from Doubleday, *The Oregon Rifles, Crooked River Canyon,* and *Disaster Creek* among them, he produced a very special kind of Western story. What makes it so special is the combination of characters who seem real and about whom a reader comes to care a great deal and Newton's fundamental humanity, his realization early on (perhaps because of his study of history) that little that happened in the West was ever simple but rather made desperately complicated through the conjunction of numerous opposed forces working at cross purposes. Yet, through all of the turmoil on the frontier, a basic human decency did emerge. It was this which made the American frontier experience so profoundly unique and which produced many of the remarkable human beings to be found in the world of Newton's Western fiction.

GUNS OF THE RIMROCK

Chapter One

For any rider who took the saddle trail down the high west wall, entering Donover Valley could be a real experience. A mighty trough, its twenty miles of graze traced in the sunlit stab of sweet mountain water—that was Donover; while all round it, marching up from timbered foothills, tall snowcaps swept away into the clouds.

Old Bob Craig, used to it as he was, caught his breath now and almost without knowing it reined his sorrel down so that he could look at that scene. The pair who rode with him halted too, without comment, their eyes more on the face of Bob than on the country before them. "Look at her, boys!" the old cattleman exclaimed softly. "Lord, you forget how beautiful she is, sometimes —even after only three days away from her!"

Neither of the others answered; but Ray Evart, looking past Bob's gray head, caught Will Ormsby's smile and the slight wink that went with it. Evart nodded, smiled a little too. Let him talk, they were saying to each other. Bob Craig had a right to. Donover was his baby.

He had been in the Valley fifteen years now—

had opened it up, in fact. The Indians were not yet all cleared out when he brought his wife and infant daughter through the gap at the eastern end; picked his site near the banks of Donover River, and laid the beginnings of his ranch—the Question Mark. There had been other troubles besides the Indians, at first. For a while rustlers had worked out of the wild rimrock country to the south, where a great, upthrust curtain of basaltic rock made a jagged break in the snowcap background. But all that was a long way in the past; and now stillness lay unbroken over that deserted upland.

And Bob Craig had survived all those early disasters—had even survived the crushing blow of his wife's death. His ranch, covering nearly half the Valley's acres, was his monument. Later, other cattlemen were to move in on the range he had opened, and the town of Fowler would spring up at the farther, eastern end, on the road leading out to the county seat. And all this, from old Bob's brave beginning.

Will Ormsby said gently, "You going to spend the night up here, Bob? It's not getting any earlier, you know."

The rancher came out of his mood with a start, and laughed at himself. "Sorry, Will. I'm afraid I got a crush on this old Valley!"

"Don't have to tell us that!"

They put their broncs on down the trail, Bob ahead with his foreman, Ray Evart, stirrup to stirrup with him. Ormsby, owner of the Box O brand lying south and east of the Question Mark, brought up the rear.

"Those white-faced bulls will graze like kings in Donover," Bob said proudly. "They're costing us a pretty penny, but the stock they breed will be worth it."

"Right," Ray Evart agreed. He had been Bob's ramrod for two years now—a big young man, with a weight of hard muscle in his arms and shoulders, and clear eyes above the dark, flat planes of his face. Ray had known only work since he was a lad. He worked hard, too, and in that way alone had gained the cow savvy it took for a man so young to rod a spread the size of the Question Mark. Besides, he was a fighting man, and old Bob liked that. "You made a good bargain on the bulls," Evart said now, "you and Will both. It was well worth a three-day ride."

"And I didn't figure I wanted to take a look at them!" Bob admitted. "Well, I'm glad you and Will talked me into it; I'd be sore if you'd let that stock be sold for any other range than Donover." That was old Bob, too—stubborn, resistant to change until others forced it on him, and then as likely as not pleased with the results.

But there was one alteration afoot now in his
Valley that Bob would never accept. As they rode
down the trail in the stillness of the afternoon,
Ray Evart's thoughts turned to that develop-
ment. It put a frown of caution across his forehead.

Not many miles before them the broad arc of
the creek showed silver. Taking its start from
the thinnest film of a waterfall, up the Valley's
northern wall, it tumbled and grew and slowed,
and added to itself the waters of tributary streams;
so that, by the time it reached level ground, it
was a fair-sized river that cut a scimitar stroke
including nearly a fourth of the Valley floor in its
bend. The stream left Donover finally by way of
a narrow gorge it had cut in the western wall, to
the right of the trail as they came down now into
the cup. Just ahead, the trail forded it at one of
its shallowest points; and it was there that the
danger to the peace of the Valley centered.

Ray Evart suggested: "Maybe we had better
turn out soon, Bob, and avoid the crossing."

"No!" Bob's face had suddenly gone tight with
anger. "I'm damned if I will! You think I'm afraid
of that rabble?"

Evart shook his head patiently. "Of course not.
But they stayed clear of Fowler, after we told

them; it seems only fair that we leave them alone, too. It does no good for the cattlemen to get their goats by making traffic through their territory."

"This is a public road!" Bob retorted, shoving aside his arguments. "I see no reason to turn out of it."

Ray shrugged. The fact was that Bob had been king of Donover too long to admit, now, that there was any spot in all its length where it was not safe or proper for him to go.

This corner behind the river's bend was the poorest land in the Valley, the soil thin and broken by spurs thrown out by the hill rim backing it. Leading as it did into the roughs at the foot of the wall where straying cattle could easily be lost and recovered only with difficulty, the ranchers had tended to leave it undeveloped. And because it had gone unwanted by the cattle element, another race of men had seized the opportunity to get a toehold for themselves in Donover.

And now, as they came down out of the last of the foothills, the three cattlemen saw about them the marks of that encroachment. The thin acres had been marked off by barbwire fencing, and given over to the plow; its furrows scarred and checkered what had once been open range. Spotted across the fields were the meagre homes of the nesters—mere shacks, smoke streaking against the blue of the sky from stovepipe chimneys. Washing flapped from clotheslines here and there.

Ray, looking at his boss, saw an intense scorn wrinkling old Bob's lips. Scorn, and anger at those who would do this to his Valley! Glancing back, he saw no expression at all on the face of Will Ormsby. Will was not so old as Bob—though there were wings of gray forming at the temples of his fine, square-cut face—but he had learned at least to keep his emotions under a better check than Bob could manage, for all his years of living close to the nub of danger.

Evart could share Bob's feelings. The beauty of the snowcapped ranges—the very brightness of the afternoon sky—seemed dulled by the ugly scars that farming had laid across the land here. It grew even worse as they finally approached the fording of the creek, and the trail dipped toward the muddy, shallow water.

The nestors, forbidden the cattle town of Fowler up the Valley, had started here a settlement of their own. A few shirt-tail merchants had followed them in, thrown up cheap jerry-built stores where they catered to the trade of the poverty-stricken farm people. There was a grogshop, set up in a dugout scooped from the mud bank, with a blanket hung for a door. All in all, the place had not over half a dozen buildings—a nameless settlement that old Bob had once scornfully dubbed "Squatter Town"—and for the cattle element, Squatter Town it had remained.

Just where the trail dipped down to the edge of the water, a big cottonwood overhung the bank. As the three cowmen threaded their way past ratty buildings and approached that crossing, they caught sight for the first time of a silent knot of men grouped in the shadow of the tree, watching them.

Will Ormsby pulled abreast of the others. "What's this ahead?" he said quietly. "A reception committee?"

"I think they want to make talk," Ray agreed. "Wonder what's troubling them?"

"They needn't think I'll take anything off that crowd," said old Bob coldly. "We're armed. I don't see any guns on them."

"Nothing to worry about, then," the foreman answered shortly. "Come on."

There were about a dozen in the group, and they fanned out slightly as the riders approached. Their leader was a man in his early thirties—a short, broad-shouldered redhead who showed the cording of muscle along his sunbrowned forearms as he stood, clenched fists on hips. They rode directly up to this man, and halted.

Ray Evart laid a glance along the mud bank, at the buildings of the settlement. He noticed a woman in a faded calico dress standing in front of the shanty that served as a general store, her thin shoulders weighted forward by an armload of packages. Then he saw that she was really not more than a girl, who had been fined down and coarsened by killing work. She was following the scene under the cottonwood with something like alarm in her face. The storekeeper had stepped to the door behind her and was watching, too.

A man came out of the grogshop dugout, jerking back sharply as he saw Ray's glance swing to him. He let the blanket he had pushed aside drop partway, but still looked out on the scene past the edge of it; and Ray could see him plainly.

Something about the man interested Evart. He was not a farmer. He had on a cheap gray sack suit, that hung loosely over a gaunt frame, and wore a battered gray felt on his head. Everything about him had a strangely gray and pinched look; even his thin face might have been dusted with grayish powder.

Ray Evart did not know the man, but he did not look like the type one would have expected to find in Squatter Town. And he seemed inordinately interested in what was going on out there under that creek-bank cottonwood.

It was Bob Craig who spoke first, breaking a silence that had begun to weigh heavily against the wash of wind in the leaves. "Well, Riley," he clipped, "what's on your mind? We're in a hurry."

The Irishman did not change expression. Fists still on hips, feet apart, he met the look of the cattleman levelly. "You'd better not be in too all-fired a hurry to talk to us," he said. "We won't be put off—now that we've got three of you to answer to us. What's it to be—war?"

"You're talking nonsense!" old Bob snorted. "The cattlemen stood aside three years ago and let you take over here. If we had wanted war we'd have started it then, wouldn't we?"

Tim Riley said sharply, "What happened three years ago cuts no ice now. Don't change the subject!"

Bob drew himself up, real anger in him. "Don't take that tone with me!" he retorted.

"Now, hold on, Bob," Will Ormsby put in quickly. To Tim Riley he said quietly, "Maybe you'd better tell us in plain language what you're getting at. The cattlemen have never wanted trouble with your end of the Valley; we don't want it now."

Riley eyed him with head ducked forward. "Just like a cowman!" he sneered. "Talk fair—and fight dirty! Broken wire and burning buildings make more noise than all the fine words you use to cover up with!"

Bob Craig cursed suddenly, and jerked the reins. "I got no time to listen to insults," he stated flatly; and with that he whirled his bronc, shoved past the knot of farmers and down the brief drop to the stream. Will hesitated, then shrugged and went after him. Only Ray Evart stayed.

There was a pucker of doubt on the foreman's dark forehead, a thoughtful narrowing of his blue eyes. He turned and reined quickly after his boss, started to call: "Wait a minute, Bob!" And then something happened.

The stone was not very big, but its aim was true. It streaked past Ray's head so close that he felt the wind of it, and there was an ugly thud as it landed. Old Bob's hat flew off his silvered hair; one hand started weakly up toward his temple. Then, with a groan, the old man toppled sideways from the saddle and landed heavily at the edge of the stream.

The cowardliness of the act sent fury sweeping through Ray Evart. He leaped from the saddle, went down the bank and knelt at the side of the rancher. Craig looked very old and very thin as he lay there in the mud. There was mud on his clothes, blood on his temple where the rock had hit him. He was unconscious.

Will had dismounted too and joined Evart. None of the nesters had moved. With a cold fury

gripping him, Ray gave the old man into the hands
of Will Ormsby and then got slowly to his feet,
turned and walked back up the slope. His face
was hard and chiseled, and there was no mercy in
him. "Who did that?" he demanded.

No one answered. The men faced him, uncom-
promising, unyielding. Evart's rage leaped hotter.
"Who did it?" he repeated. "Which of you is low
enough to stone an old man?" He turned on the
leader. "Was it you, Riley?"

"Suppose it was," the other countered, flipping
the red hair from his eyes with a toss of the head.
"Just what would you do about it?"

"I'll show you," Ray answered quietly. Already
he was shucking his coat and gun belt, throwing
them aside, coming toward Riley with hands balled
into fists. "I'll show you, if you're man enough to
stand up to me!"

"You bet—cowman!" The redhead had fallen
into a crouch, waiting, eager, his own fists clenched
and ready. "Come right ahead!"

Chapter Two

Riley was shorter than Ray Evart, but he was quick. Almost before the ramrod had set himself for it a savage punch came over and caught him in the face. Ray stopped, shaking his head, and Riley charged in on him. But Evart stood and met him with a chopping right that had all his added size and weight behind it. Riley went back on his heels, and the cowman stepped forward and swung hard with his left. The redhead twisted sidewards, stumbled and dropped heavily.

It almost looked as though the fight were over before it had started, and the ring of nesters surged forward ominously. But Riley was not out. He had one knee under him now and he pushed quickly to his feet, waving them back. He stood crouched, eyeing his opponent from under the wild red shock of hair. One eye was bruised, already swelling as he lunged forward again.

With those first two blows, Evart had known he had the man bested. Riley was not big enough, heavy enough; he knew less about fighting than the Question Mark foreman. The realization quickly damped the hot anger that had pushed Ray on into this fight; but Riley was not ready to quit yet. He was game. He closed in, gave Evart another blow against the right ear that made his whole head ring. Then they were toe to toe in the mud, slugging.

Ray sank a fist wrist deep into the redhead's body, and saw the eyes glaze slightly. "Cut it out," he begged, just loud enough for his opponent to hear. "I don't want to have to kill you, Riley."

"You go to hell!" the other gritted, and came back with a one-two that rocked Evart. The nester bored in after it, pounded Ray's face and brought blood spurting from his nose; and at that the crowd yelled approval.

It brought Ray's anger surging again. No holding back now—no pulling of punches! Riley retreated before him as he opened up with all the power he could put behind his blows. The nester stumbled back into the crowd, that scrambled out of his way. Evart followed in, gave him a couple of jolts that rammed his shoulders up against the trunk of the cottonwood.

For a long second Riley braced himself there, panting, with the crowd shouting him on. Evart waited. Then the redhead bunched his muscles and pulled away, started toward the cowman on legs that tottered slightly. One eye was puffing; there was blood on his cheek where Evart's knuckles had torn open a gash.

Determined to finish the fight before the game redhead insisted on turning it into a slaughter, Ray braced his spread legs and gathered his body for a last telling punch. He held his arm while Riley came at him; let him get over one wild swing that still had a sting to it when it landed high on his body. Then Evart unleashed his right fist in a long, looping arc, straight for the point of the man's stubborn jaw.

It landed solidly, with a crushing shock that ran up Evart's arm in numbing agony. Riley's head snapped back, hard; he crumpled without a sound, hit the mud and lay there unmoving.

Ray Evart stepped back, shaking his fingers to get some feeling into them, while he let a challenging look slide over the faces of the other men. They stood there, silent now, glaring, yet not offering to move against him. Then Evart glanced over his shoulder and saw the reason why.

Behind him, Will Ormsby was standing with a look of strong distaste on his features, but with a six-shooter steady in his hand, giving the nesters warning that they had better not try to interfere. Catching Evart's eye, he jerked his head shortly. "We'd better go," he muttered.

Ray shrugged, and stenched his bleeding nose on one shirt sleeve as he leaned to pick up again the discarded coat and gun belt. As he straightened with them in his hand, a scream ran thinly in the still air below the cottonwood. He looked quickly. The girl over by the store had dropped her bundles and was hurrying down to the river bank. She pushed her way through the ring of nesters, threw herself down beside Tim Riley's motionless form and put her thin arms around him. She was sobbing bitterly, rocking his battered head against her breast. When she looked up at Ray Evart the tears were wet on the girl's sunburnt cheeks.

"You—you bully!" she sobbed, her eyes sultry, her mouth long with misery. "You big brawling lout! Why can't—can't you fight someone that's got a chance against you?"

Ray met her look with a wooden expression on his face. There seemed nothing he could say, although her wretched anger made him wish for words that would do some good. He looked for a wedding ring on her hand, but there was none. She wasn't Riley's wife, then—just some skinny, overworked farm girl who thought a lot of the little Irishman.

Will Ormsby said, "Come on, Evart! What good can you do?"

Ray shrugged, turned his back on the sobbing girl and the nesters and walked over to the place where Will was waiting with the horses, and with old Bob who was now recovering consciousness.

He threw his coat over the saddle; the bullet-studded belt and holstered gun were in place again around his lean, flat hips.

In dead silence, except for the rustle of cottonwood branches and the small sounds of the creek, Ray and Will helped old Bob Craig onto the back of his sorrel, then mounted their own horses. The creak of saddle leather and splash of iron hoofs through the stream bed built the first sounds across the tense quiet. Then they were up the opposite bank, beyond the cottonwoods and the willows that dragged their fronds along the surface of the creek.

A hundred rods or so beyond, Ray Evart turned once to look behind him. "I wonder," he said, "if they'd dare to come after us?"

"They won't," Will Ormsby decided promptly. "With all the talk they made, not one of them has a spoonful of courage in him except that fellow Riley —and you settled him for the time being. You settled him pretty definitely, I'd say."

"Don't talk about it," Evart grunted shortly. The nose bleed had stopped, but there was still a guilty, sick feeling in him as he thought again of that performance.

Will told him, "Sure," as though he sensed the thoughts that troubled Evart. He added sourly, "It was a little too bad, though, that you had to beat up the wrong man."

Evart whipped a startled look around at him. "The wrong man?" he repeated. "You mean— Riley didn't throw that stone?"

"Of course not. It was the one standing next to him. I saw it."

Angrily, Ray demanded: "Then why the hell couldn't you have told me?"

"You didn't give me much time," Will pointed out, his voice calm and reasonable. "You put the thing up to Riley and he was too much a man to deny it, the way you came at him. The fight was over before I could say a word."

The Question Mark ramrod could not answer that, and a sense of humiliation engulfed him—an angry shame at having beaten a smaller man than himself and, furthermore, without cause. He scowled, trying to shrug the feeling away with no success.

In this time, Bob Craig had said nothing. Walking his sorrel between the others, straight in the saddle, there was a severity and pride to the old rancher that mud-drenched clothes, and the bloodstain in his silvery hair, could not lessen.

Will Ormsby turned to the old man now, as though to divert the conversation to pleasanter channels. "How you feeling, Bob?" he asked. "Think they hurt you bad?"

Without turning his gaze from directly ahead of

him, Bob Craig spat. He said one word, and it was vibrant with feeling: "Swine!"

As though not choosing to hear him, Will said: "I think when we get to town you better have Doc take a look at you. Wash the mud out of that dent and maybe put something on it."

Craig did not reply.

The southern foothills loomed very near at their left, as the river dropped behind them in the heat haze of afternoon. Cattle dotted the lush range—mostly Ormsby's Box O beef, in this section. Craig's Question Mark graze lay generally north and east, covering the larger half of the valley and controlling the best water and grass. The Anchor, the Y Bar—the other brands—were in back of Ormsby's spread, farther toward the eastern rim. Fowler, which was the Valley's town, lay that way too.

Ray Evart said, "There's something behind all this that don't show at the surface."

"What do you mean?" Bob Craig demanded.

"Those nesters weren't just talking. Something's happened in the three days we've been gone. They're plenty sore about it—but we wouldn't give them a chance to explain."

"Nonsense!" The old man's eyes snapped fire. "Don't tell me you paid any attention to that wild talk of Riley's?"

Evart shook his head in puzzlement. "They spoke of buildings being burnt, and a fence destroyed. Sounded to me as though they meant it."

"What are you saying?" Wrath shook old Bob's voice. "You—a cattleman! You'd actually listen to their insinuations? You think that any rancher in Donover Valley would be insane enough to start a war?"

"I only say we should wait until we know what we're talking about," Evart answered his boss shortly. "We've been away a few days, and a lot could have happened—"

Will Ormsby's quiet voice cut in on them suddenly. "Look up ahead!"

Two men on horses flanked the trail, waiting and watching unmovingly while their broncs cropped at hock-deep grass. Both were armed, and in addition to six-shooters they had saddle-guns slung in scabbards. One even drew a carbine out and held it ready, but as the three drew nearer he recognized them and slid the weapon back into its sheath.

Ormsby said at the same moment, "Why, it's Frank Simmons, and Reese—a couple of my boys. Looks like a guard on the trail!"

The riders touched hat brims as their boss approached. They looked gaunt and tired, beard stubbles darkening their faces. "What's up?" the Box O rancher demanded.

"Plenty, boss," Frank Simmons told him with grim weariness. "Glad to hell you're back to take over. Gus Jorgenson and us boys have been holding up your end as best we could, but we need you here."

Ormsby looked from one tight face to the other. "Where is Gus?" he asked. Jorgenson was his second in command.

"We're all out riding—guarding the river line. Want to be on hand in case anything more should break!"

Ray Evart shifted in the saddle, throwing his weight over onto one booted foot, and, bringing up the other leg, curled it across the horn. Hunched there like that, easy and graceful, with his big hat thumb-prodded back from his dark forehead, he showed little of the uneasy dread that was in him. He swung his glance swiftly over the faces of his two riding companions, waiting for the scene's effect on them.

Will said: "Go on, Frank. Start at the beginning."

Simmons shook his head. "Hard to do. Well, no, I guess it begun yesterday morning, early. That's when Bill Pine says a couple of them nesters from the roughs come into his store at Fowler and tried to buy him out of ammunition. He wouldn't sell to them, of course, and the nasty way they talked got him scared; so after they'd gone he hunted up Harry Yates who was in town with a couple of his riders, and told him. It made Harry suspicious, and he and the boys took out and caught up with the nesters. I guess they had words. In the middle of it somebody went for a gun; powder was burned, and Dick Thomas caught him a bullet."

Will Ormsby exclaimed: "They killed him?"

"No—just winged him some. After that the nesters hit out for their camp. When we learned about it a bunch of us got together and headed for there, and they met us at the ford with a bullet or two and said they'd drop the first cowman that crossed the river."

"It begins to shape up," Ray Evart said. "That's the situation we just now rode into, back yonder. But why? What got into those people, to start a thing like this?"

The rider shook his head. "They claim it was us started it. Somebody had burned Chet Black out the night before—he's the one had that place on the flats right across from your north range, Mr. Craig. A gang busted down his wire, threw a gun on him and put the torch to the house and barn. Told him to take his family and get out of the Valley. They was cattlemen, he says."

"It's a lie!" old Bob pronounced sharply. "Does he dare name any names?"

"No. He claims he didn't get a look at their faces. But I hear somebody from this side of the river's been over to investigate, and they saw the work that was done, all right. Though no cowman's spoke up to admit it was his doing."

Will Ormsby said drily, "They won't, either. No one will lay claim to a move like that, but there may be some who'll be thinking it wasn't a bad idea . . ."

"Nonsense!" old Bob Craig exploded, laying about him with his steely look. "We ranchers have kept the peace, when at any time we could have moved in and driven that scum out of the Valley. It's just not our way . . . No, this is a blind for some deviltry they themselves are planning. We got to look out that they don't try, under cover of it, to move right across the river and onto our range."

At that Ormsby's other rider, Reese, cleared his throat and spoke for the first time. "You better tell them what happened last night, Frank," he grunted sourly.

"I was aiming to show them," Simmons answered. He jerked his horse around, pointing. "It ain't far, boss. You better see for yourself."

A compelling sense of disaster rode with them, as the five horsemen jingled southward through the still of the afternoon, not speaking. After a half mile or so they made the crest of a wooded rise and then worked single file down into the hollow beyond it. Here they reined up and for a long moment no one broke the silence.

Will Ormsby had lost a dozen head of Box O stock—white-faces, all prime beef. In silent, bloated humps they lay under the hot sun, already beginning to give off the sour odor of death. Flies swarmed on them. Rifle bullets had picked them off, in a senseless slaughter.

"I noticed this bunch grazing here myself, just a few days ago, boss," Frank Simmons declared. "They ain't been dead more'n twenty hours. Happened during the night."

Ray Evart looked at Will, and saw the rancher's face drained to a sickish pallor, jaws clamped so tightly that they set the bunched muscles quivering. As Ray watched, Will Ormsby parted his lips to speak, but the sound that came out was so choked and smothered by emotion that he shut them again with the words unspoken.

The Box O rancher sat like that, one hand clenching the horn as though he needed that to hold him upright, and the knuckles of that hand were white beneath the skin.

Reese said: "These ain't the only ones. The Question Mark lost a bunch, too, Mr. Craig—shot down the same way."

Then old Bob Craig found his voice, and it came

out in a lash of fury. "The rabble! Mad dogs—that's what they are! And you, Evart, trying to argue for them; I hope you're satisfied now. This ought to show you the kind of scum we've been dealing with!"

Ray did not try to answer, for there would be no use in words now and the shock of what he had seen caused a numbness in him. He only met Craig's look levelly, and sober-faced. Even with the blood smeared across his hair and beard, the old cattleman was handsome in his wrath.

Bob turned on Ormsby. "I'm for riding to Fowler now and getting the straight on everything that's been happening. After that we'll make talk with the Anchor and the Y Bar and the others and see what's to be done. I for one ain't taking this lying down!"

Ormsby had control of himself now. He nodded curtly, told Reese and Simmons: "You boys keep on with what you're doing, and I'll send out a relief. Patrol this line between the breaks and the northern edge of the Box O graze, and if a one of that crowd from beyond the river sticks his nose on this side—well, you'll know what to do!"

"Right, boss!" Ormsby's riders touched hat brims again and, grim of face, rode off. A look told that they understood their orders.

Ray Evart said quietly, "I still think you're

making a mistake."

With an oath, old Bob whirled on him. "You've said that about once too often, Evart," he snapped. "Don't do it again! You've made me a good foreman for these last two years, but there's others to be had. Just remember that!"

"You won't fire me." There was icy amusement in Ray's smile as he said it. "Before long you'll come to your senses about this. It's just that you've had your way in Donover so long you can't stand for anything to go against you—"

Bob turned his back. "Come along, Will," he said to the other rancher. "We've wasted enough time talking!"

Chapter Three

Ray Evart watched them go, and there was the beginning of anger in him. He fought that down. That was the trouble with this Valley already— too much emotion and blind feeling ruling the hearts of men. Tempers too short, rivalries that could flame too high upon the least of fuel.

Silence had fallen again over the hollow where Evart sat his bronc alone. The dead cattle lay about, incredibly still. The buzzing of flies sounded loud and harsh; and a ground wind came down the face of a wooded slope above the hollow, soughing through the tree tops. A flock of crows took sudden flight from the tossing branches, flung themselves across the wind in a black chorus of croaking cries.

Watching their flight, Evart dug out tobacco and paper and idly built a smoke. His thoughts were far from the thing his hands were doing. What could it mean, he asked himself—this storm that had gathered and broken here in the few hours that he had been away? What madness had seized all the men of both factions in Donover Valley?

He shook his head, shoved the finished cigarette

34

between his lips and heeled a match to life. As he bent to the flame cupped between hard palms a doe broke from the upward growth of the slope and came bounding through brush and rocks, toward the lower level of the hollow.

Suddenly Evart dropped match and quirly, and with the same movement the reins were in his hands. His gelding leaped under the sudden bite of blunted rowels. Ray put it quickly across the rising floor of the hollow and then the slope of the hill was lifting sharply beneath him.

At the edge of the trees halfway up he leaned from the saddle and saw at once where a horse had stood, rein anchored. There was a scuffing of the pine needles, too, made by high-heeled boots in the time that a man had waited there, nearly motionless, before his lifting into saddle had frightened the birds and sent them in panic from the tree top just above his head.

Ray Evart saw all this in a brief second, and also the trail the man had left in going from there. It led directly up the face of the hill, and at once Evart put his bronc in that direction. Ducking branches that came whipping at his head, he had soon reached the place where the frightened deer had broken cover before the other's advance.

That first bronc had taken the rough going at an easy pace, its rider not yet aware that he was being followed. But Evart speeded his own toiling pony, and suddenly the trees opened and a clearing showed ahead. And at the other edge of that bare stretch he saw the fugitive not two hundred yards ahead of him.

In the same moment the latter became aware of his pursuer, for he turned in the saddle and threw a look behind. Faces were not discernible at that distance, but something about the figure had already identified it. Ray Evart had seen the man just once before, and that for only brief moments —yet he knew beyond doubt it was the same unknown who had shown himself at the doorway of the grog-shop back there in Squatter Town.

By his clothes and the strange, dusty gray pallor of his face, Ray Evart had known then that the stranger was no nester; and though he could not see the face now, by the clothes he identified this man who had spied on the cattlemen in the hollow where the slaughtered Box O beef lay. The stranger must have trailed them from the river, unseen—why, Ray could not imagine.

After one glimpse, the fugitive had turned about in saddle again and his bronc spurted forward as the spurs rammed home. The screen of smaller trees fringing the other rim of the clearing received him, in full flight.

Evart had never halted in his pursuit, and moments later he too struck the tangle of trees and brush beyond the clearing. It was rough going there —cedar and lodgepole grew thick, and catclaw reached to snag an unprotected face. At places the growth was so dense the gelding had literally to hurl itself at it to break through.

Presently he was at the crest of the hill and taking the downward slope beyond. The trail led him into the hollow and then sharply to the left, along a rock-bottomed gully heading up into the shouldering hills.

Whether the fugitive had any definite plan of flight or was simply tearing madly into the wildest country he could find, in an effort to throw his pursuer off the trail, it would have been hard to say. In any case, the way the rider chose was tending even higher now, ever farther back into the tangled up-country of the rimrock.

Ray pushed on, following the plain trail. His gelding was laboring with the chase, foam flying from its distended nostrils. But Evart wanted that man ahead—wanted to know from him his part in the strange turmoil that had seized Donover Valley.

He came out at the head of a gully—and heard the sudden whisper of lead sing past his ear.

The boom of a rifle and the splat of the bullet into the rocks behind him followed, almost at once. Quick reaction jerked Evart's hand on the reins

and the gelding lunged sidewards under it; and at
the same moment the Question Mark ramrod
dragged his own carbine from its saddle scabbard.
His angry eyes searched ahead for a sight of the
man who had fired at him.

He found him almost at once, although horse
and rider were half hidden in the scrub growth.
The fugitive had stopped to take the shot at his
pursuer, and perhaps also to wind his bronc after
its battle with the foothill growth. It was the wink-
ing sunlight on the barrel of his rifle as he lifted it
for another shot that had led Ray Evart's glance to
him.

Before the man could fire again Evart snapped
his own rifle to his shoulder and triggered once.

He was too hasty for accuracy, and firing up-
hill put the bullet low; but it achieved its primary
purpose of changing the other's mind. His bronc
threw up its head, deflecting the bead that the fugitive was trying to draw. In that same instant Ray
gave his gelding the spurs and it lunged forward
again, straight at the other.

Without taking that second shot, the stranger
quickly turned his bronc and fled. And Ray Evart
was right behind him, although he sensed now
that the other was mounted on a faster horse than
his own and was drawing away again.

They had climbed very high. The knife-edge of

basaltic rock that made the Valley's southern wall hung close above them. The sudden thought occurred to Evart that if the fugitive could get over that wall, through any one of the fissures that split its eroded face, he would have an excellent chance of escaping into the badlands behind it; in the old days, as Ray had often heard it told, rustlers had used that rimrock country as a base of operations when the cattlemen were fighting their first battle to hold the Valley.

The thought made Ray Evart force a last burst of speed from his bronc; and with that the trail brought him out upon a sheer pitch of barren rock. Far, far below were the lower hills, and the green of Donover Valley and the flash of its streams. And just ahead the fugitive was fighting his way precariously up the cliff face, toward a cleft that offered escape into the broken rim.

A wind sang through that slot, and the sky's blue shone dazzlingly above the jagged top of the wall. And there, high under the sky, the man on the other horse hung at the lip of nothing, with escape into the rim just yards away. Ray Evart put in his spurs and went after him.

At once his gelding was in trouble. The rocks were smooth and slick, and there was a crumbling of talus from the broken wall above that slid under pawing hoofs. For a moment Ray forgot everything else in that quick, wild struggle; only when his gelding had got its footing could he look up ahead once more.

He saw then that the fugitive had veered suddenly out of his course and was slanting sharply away from the cleft for which he had been heading a minute before. Wondering at that, Ray watched two riders appear out of the mouth of the crevice.

Evart reined in quickly, astonished at the sight of them. They, too, sawed with the leathers, and their horses reared a little in a spurt of rock dust before managing a halt. There was little time to speculate on the presence of those horsemen, though. Even as Ray stared one of them whipped a six-gun out of its holster and let a bullet fly at the Question Mark ramrod.

Quickly, Ray slipped from the saddle. His boots slid in the loose rock as he lit, and he went forward to his knees, catching himself with his left hand while with the right he kept a firm hold on the carbine, that he had drawn from its scabbard when he leaped. He felt surer with the ground under him —treacherous, sliding stuff though it was—than he had in the saddle with a thousand foot drop yawning under his gelding's uncertain hoofs.

But the bronc, frightened by the clap of the six-gun in the thin air, had bolted and plowed on a few yards through the loose stones, and Ray was left unprotected from the gun that had fired at him. A boulder resting on the steep face of the slope offered its shelter a dozen feet away, and throwing himself flat Ray Evart rolled and scrambled for it, making its shadow just as another gunshot clapped and a slug whined over him.

He flopped around at full length and got the rifle into position for firing, prone.

He had lost his hat, and the wind down from the cleft jerked at his hair and blew it into his eyes, interfering with his sighting. He had no particular desire to kill, not knowing who these men were or why they were firing at him. But those bullets had both come too close for his liking and it seemed evident to him that they had been meant to score. Even now one of the riders took another shot and the lead spanged off the face of the boulder, whining away toward the deep blue of the heavens.

Evart moved quickly, threw a snap shot into the mouth of the cleft, and rolled back to safety before that gun could find him. In that brief second he gained a good picture of the thing: One of the men had dismounted, and was using his gun against Evart from the ground. The other had disappeared, and Ray guessed that he had taken both horses and gone farther up into the slot with them, perhaps to tie them and come back to help in the fight.

As for the unknown rider who had brought him into this, in that short view Evart had had no glimpse of him. A thin straggle of timber clinging to the cliff's face made a dim green cloud, off to the right and lower than Evart's shelter. Since the fugitive hadn't made it into the cleft for which he had been heading, the best guess would be that he had veered instead for the shelter of that growth. At least there was no sign of him on the slope of talus.

Ray Evart levered a fresh shell into his rifle's smoking chamber. The man at the mouth of the notch above him had not fired again; he was evidently holding his fire, waiting for a good shot. Across the wild slope a strange, deceptive stillness had fallen.

Slowly, Evart got his knees under him and came up into a crouch, a position which put his head just below the top of the protecting boulder. He waited like that, hugging the sun-bright face of the rock and listening, but still hearing only the steady voice of the wind through the notch.

When the silence had run on longer than his patience, he began to wonder if the pair at the cleft had pulled out and left him. Moving cautiously, he straightened up enough to bring his eyes above the level of the boulder, for a quick look.

The startling slam of a revolver shot greeted him, and he fell back with rock dust smarting in his eyes. The men had not gone. One at least had been waiting there, with equal patience, ready to place lead at any point where he might show himself. Now, as that bullet screamed off the top of the boulder just inches from where his head had showed, Ray heard a shout break out in triumph.

The man thought that slug had got him; and Ray did not give him time to think again. Discarding the rifle as too awkward, he quickly had his six-gun dug out of leather and was rounding the edge of the boulder in a leap, charging straight up toward the mouth of the cleft. He came face to face with the man who had fired the shot; the latter, who had started legging it down through the crumbled rock on the tail of his bullet, pulled up short at sight of Evart. He had been sure that slug had landed home. There was an expression of amazement on his bearded face now; the gun in his hand still dribbled smoke.

His surprise only lasted a fraction of a second. Already he was crouching and whipping the gun into line for another shot. But Ray was ready first and his own weapon jerked to pressure on the trigger. The man stumbled; the gun dropped from his fingers and went skittering down over the rocks.

Then his knees buckled and he fell headlong, slid heavily through the loose stuff. As Ray watched he struggled to his feet, took two or three uncertain steps; then fell again and came rolling over and over down the slope to bring up not a dozen feet from Evart's boulder. He flopped over and lay there on his back, face to the sky, and blood marked a trail where his body had plowed through the loose talus.

Ray did not look at him then. He had already switched his attention back to the mouth of the cleft, and now the other man came running out of it, gun in hand. Not giving him time to fire, Evart met him with a quick shot that chipped rock from the wall at his side.

The other ducked back and raised his gun. Evart, legs spread and back braced against the boulder, pulled trigger again and heard a howl of pain. And the man dropped his gun, clutching at one arm while his mouth widened in a round O of agony.

Ray called up to him: "Lift your hands and back away from that gun, fellow, if you don't want another one and a little closer into center next time—"

But suddenly the man turned and bolted; and Ray let him go. He waited, hearing the quickly receding sounds of running footsteps, up the rocky throat of the cleft; and then hoofbeats started, distantly, and faded out. From his panicky haste, it seemed hardly likely that Evart could expect further trouble from that one.

There was still the man he had killed. Slowly, Ray walked over and stood looking down at him. He was sure now that this was no one he had ever seen before. Thoroughly nondescript, in worn range clothes and with a two-day beard on his not-too-intelligent face, he could have been a drifting range tramp—except for the puzzling fact of his presence in this rimrock country.

It needed explaining; and gingerly Evart holstered his gun and knelt to examine the man's pockets. A knife, a little change, part of a plug of chew—nothing to give a hint. And then, in a pocket of the blood-soaked shirt, Ray's questing fingers discovered a fold of note paper.

He drew it out, opened it.

It was finger-marked and much read—a letter, dated a month before but with no heading and no address. He glanced over it, then went back and read it all again, carefully, and with a sense of holding something of great importance.

Legg (the letter read):

I'm sending this through the usual channels and hoping it gets to you in time. I want you to come in with me. Donover is a sweet proposition, getting sweeter. Old Craig is no fool, despite what you may have heard, but he is hotheaded and we can handle him. Duncan can be trusted OK. He is in solid with the cattlemen, has everything lined up and will work with us to the hilt.

Get some of the good men—Warman, Blant, Lou Shargan: You'll know who we want. Meet me at the usual place within three weeks, if you're coming. I'll wait for your sign.

Sid Roberts

Chapter Four

Riding slowly in toward town, Craig and Will Ormsby had little to say to one another. The stunning weight of the thing that had struck the Valley in their absence seemed to have settled heavily on both of them, and words came with difficulty.

It was a good two hours before sunset when they entered town. Fowler was no metropolis, consisting only of a small cross-hatching of streets and the low one- and two-storied buildings that lined them. Today the place looked deserted, even more so than usual. A stagnant air of waiting hung over it; and when the hoofs of their horses kicked up the dust it hung for a long time without settling, or being dissolved and swept away by any breeze.

Old Bob said, "I don't see anyone here. I think I'll head for the Question Mark."

"No," Will objected. "I want the doc to look at you. That's a mean cut you've got."

"Fiddlesticks!" Bob muttered. Yet he rode with Ormsby to the shack, a block off Main Street, where Doc MacGowan lived and carried on his practice; and here they received a mild surprise. Three saddled horses were tied to the picket fence in front of the cottage, and from the sound of voices through the open windows a small meeting was in progress.

"Harry Yates is here," Will remarked, putting his glance over the trio of saddled broncs. "And that's Sol Bingham's roan. I wonder what's up?"

They dismounted, tied in alongside the others, and walked up to the house. The wooden gate's creaking brought someone to the screen door, and as they reached the porch they saw that it was Sol Bingham. He stared at them dull-wittedly a moment, before he recognized the newcomers; then the Anchor owner grunted his surprise and quickly swung the screen open for them, drawing his huge bulk aside to let them through.

At the round table in the center of the room, Doc MacGowan was redoing the bandage on a puncher's arm; bottles, scissors, and cloth littered the table top and the smell of iodine was strong in the breathless air. The doctor straightened, brushing white hair back from a damp forehead, to greet Will and Bob. And over at the fireplace Harry Yates took his elbow from the mantel and came alert.

Yates started to say, "Well, I'm glad to see *you*," but the doctor cut in on him. "Bob! You're a hell of a bloody mess! What have you done to yourself?"

Old Craig scowled. "It's nothing," he muttered.

But Doc MacGowan would not be put off. He told the puncher he had been working on, "I guess I'm finished with you, Dick. Just keep your arm in that bandage and try not to use it too much, and I'll take another look in a couple of days . . . Now, let Bob have this chair a few minutes so I can work on him."

Dick Thomas went over by the mantelpiece to talk with his boss, and old Bob let himself be steered into the chair at the table. MacGowan clucked in sympathy as he inspected the torn scalp; and while he went to the kitchen for a basin of warm water out of the kettle on the stove, and clean rags to bathe the wound, Will Ormsby told the other three what had happened.

"It was a rock," he said. "That Squatter Town crowd tried to stop us, and one of them threw it when our backs were turned. A bit harder and it might have killed him."

Yates swore. His voice could take on a very harsh edge when he was angry, and he was angry now. "You hear him?" he demanded. "First Dick Thomas, and then this. I tell you there's nothing that gang will stop at—not if they'd stone an old man! *Now* what do you have to say about it, Sol?"

Big Sol Bingham shifted his weight uncomfortably and looked uneasily around him. "I don't know, Harry," he answered miserably. "I'm a peaceable man—you all know that. And we've always managed, with those nesters staying on their own side of the creek. I hate now to think of it coming to war—"

"Well, it's come!" Yates told him shortly. "But you're just too damn wool-headed to see it. You mark my words, it's either them or us now. I say run the rabble out or one of these times they'll catch us napping."

"Just a moment, Harry," Will put in. "There's such a thing as being hasty, too. You both have arguments. Let's put our heads together on this, instead of calling each other names we might regret later."

Harry Yates turned his black anger on Ormsby, forgetting the unhappy Sol Bingham. "Go right ahead!" he grunted. "Stick up for the half-wit. Trouble with you, Ormsby, you're afraid to hurt people's feelings. Well, I reckon there's gonna be feelings hurt plenty—and toes stamped on, too—before this is over. And it's gonna be every man looking to his own interests." He added, "As for me, I'm just a little sick to my stomach from standing here listening to this guy and his drivel about still trying to get along peaceable." He jerked a thumb at his puncher. "Come on, Dick!"

They left, the Y Bar owner's words still stinging in the air. In the silence that followed, Bingham's look appealed to Will, but the latter was scowling at a figure in the carpet. Doc MacGowan had heard the tail end of the scene as he stood in the doorway with water and cloths in his hands; now he came into the room, set the basin on the table and began gently bathing the side of Bob's head. The water in the basin quickly turned red.

Through the open window the sound of hoof-beats started and faded out as Yates and Thomas rode away; and for a long time the silence ran on unbroken. Will Ormsby shrugged, then, and lifting his head saw the unhappiness on Sol Bingham's heavy features. He said, "Don't mind what Harry said. He's pretty much worked up, and he don't guard his tongue. I dunno, though, but what part of what he said is right—I mean about it being war. I'm near believing the same thing."

The doctor, working over old Bob, shook his head. "It beats me what's come into people," he grunted. "I may be having a lot of new business soon—from both sides of the river."

"You'd go over and help those nesters?" old Craig spoke up hotly.

"Now, look, Bob," Doc said in his quiet tone, "you know I'm the only sawbones within a day's ride of this Valley. Naturally my sympathy's with my friends—but I can't refuse help to anybody that might need it. I took an oath like that once, a long time ago."

Bob could not answer that, and he did not try; but the rope-hardened fingers of his right hand began to drum the table top angrily. After another silence, Will Ormsby spoke up.

"What about you, Sol?" he asked the Anchor owner. "You lost any stock yet—like me?" And even as he said that the memory of a hollow filled with bloated Box O carcasses showed clearly in the tightening of his face.

Sol shook his head. "No," he answered, and added apologetically: "I been kind of outa touch with things—had some work to keep me pretty close at the ranch, you know. I really didn't hear much of what was going on until Harry Yates come by today and told me. He told me you and Bob both had several head killed on you, and was goin' to take me to see for myself as soon as Dick got finished here in town. But—" he glanced unhappily through the door—"I guess he got mad and went off without me."

"Come along with me," Bob told him grimly. "I aim right now to take me a look at what the scum did to the Question Mark— Oh, quit fussing around, Doc! I ain't gonna bleed to death!"

He was already on his feet, jamming his hat on; and as a matter of fact the flow of blood from the stone's mark had ceased some time before. "I'm a patient man," he told the room in general, "and I've put up with that scum at Squatter Town for longer than many another would. But if they finally make me turn loose my wolf—they're gonna wish they hadn't! Will," he added to the Box O rancher, "you coming along?"

Ormsby shook his head. "No, guess not, Bob—got business in town. Maybe I can drop out later in the evening."

"Good. We got to talk this over. I reckon you'll want to say hello to Jan, too."

Will grinned. "I reckon."

Bob nodded curtly to the doctor, and told Sol Bingham, "Let's go."

Afterwards, Doc gave Ormsby a look and then with a sigh began putting away the stuff he had been working with. "Bob's a fine man," he observed drily, "but I do get mad at him sometimes."

Will nodded and smiled. "I know how you feel. Well," he added thoughtfully, "the old boy means a lot to Donover Valley. Damn near everything, I reckon!"

In the presence of other men, Sol Bingham did not show to the best advantage, and he knew it. He could not talk glibly; he could not order his thoughts and put them into words, or even win an argument by shouting loudly, as some men—Harry

Yates, for example—were prone to do when their own reasoning was shaky.

But he knew animals and loved them, and that counted for much in Donover Valley. The account books he struggled with during many sleepless nights in the Anchor living room were horrors of blotted figures; but his canniness and deep wisdom in range matters and care of stock made up for any lack in business sense, and the ranch generally showed a profit—at least, enough to get by.

Riding with Bob Craig now, in the golden hour before sunset, there was deep unhappiness in him. As he had told Ormsby, the events of the last two days had been lost on him in his immediate worry for a favorite mare who was having trouble with her foal. To be brought out of that all-absorbing problem to face a crisis in the affairs of the Valley had been a shock. And when Harry started yelling at him it had been more than his slow wits could cope with.

He watched the stern face of old Bob, looking to him instinctively for leadership. If the Question Mark voted for war, then he supposed war it would have to be. Bob Craig was always right. A damn good cattleman, old Bob.

Almost in sight of the home buildings they crossed trails with Jack Dalley, who was a sort of second foreman under Ray Evart. Jack touched up his gray with the spurs and came cantering to meet them, his broad face sober and tired-looking. "Gosh, I'm glad you're back, chief!" he told Bob, with the relief of one who could now dispose of too heavy a burden. He added: "Where's Evart?"

At mention of his foreman, Craig only shrugged. "Never mind that," he grunted, as though it were an unpleasant subject. "I want to see what this Squatter Town gang has done to the Question Mark."

"Oh, you've heard?" Dalley nodded grimly. "Of course," he put in quickly, "we got no real proof it was them. It happened in the night—"

"All right, all right," Bob cut him off impatiently. "Just lemme see."

The puncher showed them. They went across the rolling hills, skirted a herd of cattle bearing the Question Mark iron, and so came at last onto the sharp edge of a long hogback. They reined up there, as sunset stained the sky overhead, for from this point they could see many things. Away ahead was the flaming course of the stream, and in back of that the Valley wall with the acres of nester land at its foot.

And directly below them lay a replica of the sight old Bob had witnessed on Will Ormsby's range—the same bloated carcasses, the stench, the buzzing flies. Now Sol Bingham looked at that de-

struction—that senseless and wanton slaughter—
and through his mind a slow fire of rage began to
burn. He saw a red trail of blood telling where
one old milch cow had been only crippled by the
butchers' lead, to stagger for many yards in her
agony before merciful death had ended her misery.

His big hands clamped tight on the horn, the
Anchor owner shook his head slowly, over and over
again. "They ought to be skinned!" he exclaimed,
almost sobbing. "The men that done this ought to
have their hide jerked off them, bit by bit!"

Nobody tried to answer him. Instead, Jack
Dalley lifted one arm and pointed out across the
Valley flats, to the land beyond the river. "That
there's where this fellow Chet Black was burned
out night before last, Mr. Craig. I was over and
seen what's left—just some twisted wire and the
ruins of his buildings. He's gone now. Claims the
Question Mark drove him out."

"The lying scum!" Bob gritted. "I wish we *had*
done it, instead of leavin' one of the other ranchers to beat us to the draw; wish whichever it was
would own up so I could thank him—"

He broke off suddenly, a queer expression
building in his face; and when he spoke again
Bob's voice had a new tone in it—a sort of grim
resolve. He said: "Jack, I'll tell you what I want
you to do. You know that hundred head that's feed-

ing on the flats a half mile back of us? Take some
of the boys and round them up—tonight—and
push that cattle across the river."

Jack Dalley's mouth dropped open. He managed a choked *"What!"*

"The Question Mark is moving across the river,"
old Bob repeated levelly, "before any of those
other nesters can take over on the land where Black
was driven off. We're going into that north corner, and staying there—and we'll keep crowding
right in on every foot of ground they give up, until
we've shoved them right out of the Valley! And
we'll keep them out."

"But—but, chief!" The puncher stumbled over
the words. "Think what we might be getting into!
And if we put our beef on the flats yonder, how
we gonna keep from losing a lot of them into the
breaks?"

The old man dismissed that with a shrug. "Put
enough men with them and there won't be any
trouble. They can keep the critters out in the
open, out of the breaks; as far as that goes, who
gives a damn if we do lose a few? And if the
nesters feel like doing anything about this, they'll
change their minds fast enough if they see Question Mark backing it up with everything we've
got."

He reached out and laid a hand on the young

man's shoulder. "I'm putting it in your hands, Jack," he added soberly. "Ray Evart's not here; and even if he was I reckon he'd put up a lot of fight and give me trouble. But the men all like you, and they'll work for you. Do this tonight the way I want it done—and there could be a new job for you tomorrow."

And then, without waiting for an answer, he nodded a curt "Good night" to Sol Bingham and spurred off toward home, alone. He didn't feel like talking any more with the slow-witted Anchor owner right now, even though Sol did appear to be coming to his senses now that he'd seen that slaughtered beef. Bob had done enough arguing for one day; now it was time to act. And once he did, he had no doubts that the Valley would follow his lead quickly enough.

There was still a dull, throbbing pain where the stone had struck him. Old Bob put up a hand and touched the place, and again contemptuous anger filled him. The rabble! He had held himself back too long, shown them a greater courtesy and tolerance than they had any right to expect. He had let them stay in Donover Valley, which was cattle range and God willing always would be.

All right. If now, after all his leniency, they had decided they wanted war, he'd show them he wasn't too old to fight back. Moreover, he'd show them he could also strike first—that the cattle-men had brains as well as guns.

Occupied with these thoughts, and in a generally unpleasant mood, Bob reached the Question Mark home ranch just as gray dusk was deepening in the trough of the Valley. It was an excellent layout, the ranch house large and shaded, the barns and outbuildings newly painted and corrals in good re-pair. Bob Craig usually took pride in the knowl-edge that he had carved a fine spread out of a valley wilderness and built it up, in fifteen years, to this. But tonight he was not thinking much along such lines.

He swung out of saddle under the tamarisks in front of the house, calling to one of the boys to take care of his weary bronc. There were no lights in the house yet, though dusk was rapidly turn-ing into full night; and he saw no sign of his daughter, Jan—which pleased old Bob just as well at the moment. He wasn't yet ready to face her, or the questions he knew she would ask. Instead he strode up the steps and into the house, groped his way down the dark hall and swung open the door of the room that he used for an office.

On the threshold, he halted suddenly. A man was sitting at his desk, by the window—a man Bob had never seen before—and he looked as though he might have waited there a long time. In the dim light coming through the window the stranger's face seemed strangely pale, pasty-colored, as though dusted with gray powder; all his clothes were gray as well. He said nothing, just sat there in the growing dusk looking at old Bob, while his lean fingers toyed with a paper knife and picked out tiny scars in the polish of the desk.

Bob Craig went on into the room, closing the door behind him.

Chapter Five

And the Question Mark moved across the river, into the northwest corner, onto Chet Black's deserted homestead. In a long, dark line the herd rolled down the shallow banks, the only sounds the clatter of hoofs and horns, and the calling of punchers back and forth through the settling dusk.

Jack Dalley, in charge, rode nervously along the column and watched with particular concern the first crossing at the river. But there was no trouble there. After the leaders had been shoved over the others followed willingly enough. Jack nodded, satisfied, and put his gray forward into the water to supervise the bedding down at the other side.

Within an hour it all was done. Looking back over the job, Dalley felt well pleased with himself. He leaned to touch his cigarette to the flame of a match that the rider next to him held ready, then settled back in the hull. The other man shook out the match and both their smokes made cherry eyes in the new darkness.

"Well, Gillis," Jack observed, "that's that."

Gillis mumbled something.

"What'd you say?" Dalley demanded.

"I said I think the old man's crazy. It'll be a long time before we see the last of what we've just done here."

Jack said crisply: "I'll pretend I didn't hear that, Gillis. Craig's a good boss, who pays top wages—and if that ain't enough, you want to remember you're a cattleman! If you got any loyalty, and a pair of eyes in your head, you'll figure it out yourself that this had to come sooner or later." He reined away then, went on brusquely: "I'll send out a relief in a couple of hours. You and three others will stay with the cattle—I want you to keep an eye on these critters, and don't let anything bother 'em. Understand? I'll see you later."

Riding in to headquarters, Jack Dalley knew he hadn't been quite honest. The orders for this move had rather shocked him, too, when old Bob gave them. They still seemed unwise, or at least a little dangerous. But that was old Bob's business.

In the past hour or two he'd changed his mind about a lot of issues—mainly because of the last thing Bob had said to him. That hint had opened wide vistas of possibility. Jack had always been a plodder, and, like most unoriginal men to whom opportunity has never presented itself, had never suspected he was an ambitious man. But now

strange new thoughts were in him—pleasant
thoughts, that had a headiness like strong drink.

On the whole, he believed, he had handled things
pretty well these last few days, with Bob and his
foreman gone. This move tonight had gone off
smoothly, too. Old Bob himself had told him the
men liked to work for Jack; certainly, it did seem
that he had some of the qualities of leadership.
Most likely he would step right into the foreman's
job—if Ray Evart should get his walking papers.

What on earth had happened between Evart and
the old man? he asked himself. Something, certainly. He wondered if they had quarreled. Bob
Craig would never stand for a foreman who dis-
agreed with his policies—or at least, who did so in
open words.

Jack filed that observation away for future ref-
erence. It was the real reason why he was busily
changing his own opinions on a lot of points right
now.

Ray Evart, with the dead gunman at his feet and
the silence of the peaks around him, slowly folded
Sid Robert's note and buttoned it away into his
shirt pocket. There was much in it that puzzled
him, much that he would have to worry out when
he had the time. That part about Duncan, espe-
cially—*"Duncan is in solid with the cattlemen"*

—the cattlemen of Donover Valley, in other words. Yet Ray knew no one of that name.

There was no uncertainty, though, about Sid Roberts; the outlaw had never been known to operate before in that end of the state, but the things that he and his gang had done elsewhere were well known. Ray had read the descriptions, and heard tales of daring and merciless audacity told about Roberts and his gang. If the man Evart had killed—Legg—were a member of that gang, and if Sid Roberts were indeed there in the rimrock country, it put a wholly new complexion on the tangled affairs of Donover Valley. It had frightening implications.

Frowning at these thoughts, Ray punched the empties out of his six-gun, and then retrieved his hat and the carbine and walked over the sliding rocks to where his horse waited, reins trailing. He patted the sweating flank. The gelding, normally terror-stricken at gunfire, was so exhausted from its chase that even the battle on the ridge had not been enough to send it far.

Considering that, Ray abandoned any idea of further exploration of the rimrock, or of packing the body of Legg down to Fowler with him. His bronc simply could not manage anything more. It was going to be a slow, precarious descent anyway, and he would be doing well if he made it out of the hills by nightfall.

He struck out on foot, the bronc trailing at the reins with drooping head. Below him, on the easiest grade, was the stand of timber where the spy he had chased last disappeared. Ray approached it with caution, but soon saw that the rider had gone right on from there; he was probably far away by now, and there would be no further hope of trailing him.

Thinking about the stranger who had brought him into that gun battle on the ridge, Ray felt a certain chagrin that was directed at himself. More than ever now he wanted to get his hands on the man: first, because he still thought his suspicious actions in trailing Craig and Ormsby and himself, and spying on them, needed explanation; and second, because he had an idea the stranger had known quite well that Legg and the other man were guarding that cleft in the rimrock, and had led Ray to them in order to shake the Question Mark ramrod from his own tail. That was just a hunch, but it was a strong one.

The afternoon was waning, however, and for the present he would have to forget about hunting the stranger. So, taking the easiest way down from the steeps, Ray Evart headed for the far green of the Valley floor.

Sunset was swarming in color across the sky

when he finally rode into town, and it laid a golden sheen over the street's dust. Ray put his horse at a hitch rack where it could reach the water in a wooden trough, that had moss clinging where it overflowed. As he stepped down from the saddle, Ray noticed how the reflected crimson rippled in the surface of the water; and how the weary bronc's thrust of muzzle into it sent the colors wriggling and chasing.

There was no one at all on the street. Ray's bootheels on the wooden walk sounded very loud in his own ears, as he went along to a saloon and in through the swinging doors. Here too there was silence and emptiness, and also the sharp, sour odor of liquor. The barkeep put down his paper and came to draw him a beer.

"Quiet in town this evening," Ray observed, after the first long pull had cleared his dusty throat and taken some of the weariness from behind his eyes. "I didn't see anyone outside."

"There's no one around," the other agreed. "The ranchers haven't time for us—not now. Yates and Bingham were in a few hours ago, with Dick Thomas—the boy that got shot up over at the creek. They didn't stay long."

Ray finished his drink and set down the big glass. "Has there been any word from Joe Buckley?" he demanded.

"The sheriff?" the barkeep echoed with raised eyebrows. He made a small sound of disgust. "I reckon not! Oh, he's probably heard rumors about what's broke loose here in Donover; but the county seat's too far away—and his own seat in the jail office is a little too comfortable. Things'll have to get pretty bad before you'll see him riding all the way over to this country."

They talked awhile longer about the recent happenings. It seemed to Ray the whole mood of the Valley was one of uncertainty—of a seething anger against the nesters, tempered by doubt as to the next effective move. He could sense that there had been a general waiting for old Bob to get back from the trip outside, with Ormsby and himself— as if no definite action could be taken unless the Question Mark suggested or supported it.

He saw no point in mentioning his run-in with Sid Roberts' men, or the killing of Legg. But he did ask casually, "Mac, do you remember ever seeing a stranger around town that fit this description: rather tall, bent a little in the shoulders; pinched features and ugly sort of eye, and a very pale, sick-looking complexion? Do you recall such a man?"

Mac, the barkeep, thought a moment. "Sure don't," he said finally. "Why? Who is he?"

"That's what I'd like to know." Ray finished his second beer. "I'm full of crazy questions this evening," he added, after a silence. "Here's one more. Does the name 'Duncan' mean anything to you?"

"Nope. Never heard it in this part of the range."

"I see." The Question Mark ramrod fished out loose change to pay for his drinks. "Well," he concluded, "if you can't tell me I don't imagine anyone else could. Thanks just the same."

He knew he had left the man puzzled, but he did not feel like explaining. The important thing now was to head for the Question Mark and show old Bob the letter in his pocket, and decide what difference the news about Roberts was going to make.

Dusk was dropping quickly now as sunset faded from the sky, and already a chill had come down from the snowpeaks above the Valley. Ray Evart paused a moment on the walk in front of the saloon, reaching for tobacco sack and papers; then he lowered his hand suddenly at what he saw coming toward him through the dusty street.

There were five of them, on crowbait nags, and dressed in patched and tattered hickory shirts and levis. Their saddles were battered, the trees of some of them showing through torn leather; but the rifles they carried openly or balanced across the horns gleamed.

Evart let the smoke go. He waited, seeing that

the newcomers were heading toward him, wondering what they wanted. They were men of Squatter Town, and for them to ride into Fowler now was plenty dangerous. They knew that, too, judging from the alertness in their eyes, and the rifles in their hands, and the way they fanned out in fighting order as they reined their horses in front of Ray Evart.

The leader—a bone-thin farmer with a level eye—said to Ray: "You don't have to answer this —but I want to know if you got a doctor in this place."

Ray nodded, and answered quietly, "You'll find Doc MacGowan's house half a block down the first cross street, to your right. Can't miss it."

The other nodded curtly, made as though to ride on but hesitated. He turned back, laid a narrow look slowly up and down the length of the darkening street, finding it empty. He looked at Ray. "I dunno," he suggested slyly; "maybe you better come along and show us."

"I said you can't miss it," Ray repeated, his tone sharper. "Why should I go with you?"

One thin shoulder lifted, as the scarecrow gave a shrug. "This here is a cattle town," he grunted. "We don't want to attract the wrong kind of attention here—wouldn't like you calling out the wolves the minute our backs was turned."

"Now listen here," Ray snapped. "If you need the doc, go find him; he'll be glad to help you. Me, I got other business at the moment, and what you do is none of my concern. Now you'll have to excuse me," he ended shortly, and turned away toward his bronc at the hitch rack.

One of them said, "Hold on a minute, cowman." And to the others: "That's him right there. That's Ray Evart!"

Ray halted, faced a sudden tightening of tension in the group. He replied quickly, "Yes, I'm Evart. Why?"

"It was you beat up Tim Riley this afternoon and broke his jaw. I was there—I seen it!"

"Broke his jaw!" Evart, recalling the last crushing blow of that fight, could feel again the pain of it tingling up his arm; and he remembered now the sense he had had of something giving before it, as the nester's head rolled under the impact and his knees buckled. But he had not guessed what damage the crushing wallop might have done.

"He's been out cold ever since," the man continued. "We done everything we could, but it wasn't much; and finally, Peg Sothern talked us into coming over here to Fowler to get the doc." He added: "I'm glad now we did—because I've been itching to meet you again!"

His calloused hands caressed the wooden rifle stock as he said that; but the thin-faced man in front spoke without turning his head to look at him. "Ease up, Polk!" the leader commanded, and the other went sullen but obeyed.

Ray told them: "I'm willing to apologize for going off the handle and doing that to Riley. I learned later he wasn't guilty of the thing I accused him of. I wish you'd tell the girl that I'm sorry—Peg Sothern, did you say her name was? And you can tell Doc MacGowan to fix Tim's jaw and charge the bill to me."

"It ain't as easy as that, cowman," the man who had recognized him retorted. "You think you can crawl your way out of this—now that you ain't got anyone siding you with a gun. Well, we'll show you!"

Suddenly, as though at a signal, all but the leader of the five had thrown their legs over saddlehorns and were slipping to the ground. They did it without lowering the aim of their rifles, and now they faced Evart in a ring, crouched a little, with the muzzles of the old carbines full on him.

The thin-faced leader had not moved or said another word; he sat, gaunt and sombre, in the battered hull and watched what was shaping there. Ray, alarmed, backed away a little as the quartet started for him slowly. He was conscious of the holstered gun at his thigh, but with all those rifles trained on him there was no chance to go for it. He waited, in the thickening dusk, wondering what they had in their minds.

Then one of them darted in, his rifle poised as though to club him. Ray, whirling to meet the charge, caught a spur in a crack of the old sidewalk and stumbled; the next instant another of the men was in behind him and he felt his arms grabbed roughly, jerked back and down. The man who had made the feint with his rifle laughed and let the weapon fall again harmlessly. And after that the nester who had started it all by calling Evart's name came in toe to toe with him, and leered into the prisoner's startled face.

"You like a fair fight, don't you?" he jeered. "Or do you like it better standing up to someone who ain't got the size you have, or the weight to put into his fists? Well, there's one way to pare you down, cowman, so that an ordinary gent can handle you—and show you what it's like for once to be taking it instead of dishing it out. For example—"

The blow crashed square against Ray's unprotected face; but the latter had sensed its coming and rolled his head aside to cushion most of the shock. Landing full, the vicious punch could have given him a broken jaw like Tim Riley's. As it was, blood sprang out on his cut face, above the cheekbone.

He made no sound of pain, but hot anger was in his eyes as, helpless, he crossed looks with the man who had struck him. Up in the saddle, the gaunt leader said quietly: "That'll do now, Polk. We better be getting out of here before somebody comes."

But Polk wasn't satisfied so easily. Suddenly both his arms began pumping at Ray. Evart ducked his head, but couldn't ward off the rain of blows. Through them he heard Polk's curses, and heard the man who held his arms cry out in disgust: "Hey now, wait! Enough's enough!"

At the same time his grip on the prisoner lessened a bit, and that was all the chance Ray needed. Suddenly he bucked, jerking forward. His arms came free; the man who had held them caromed off Evart's hip and landed heavily. And Ray plunged ahead, into the startled Polk. The latter gave a squawk but moved too slowly to save himself. Ray grabbed him by the shirtfront and dragged him close to cover his own body, while with his right hand he dug for his six-gun.

"Drop those rifles," he told the rest. "You can't use them without plugging your friend, and I don't think you'd want to do that!"

He waited then, and let them think it over,

while the blood ran down into his eye from a cut on his forehead, and Polk squawled and struggled in the iron grip Ray had on him. The other nesters quickly saw there was no point in continuing the incident; besides, they all felt a certain shame at the attack their companion had made.

As soon as he saw their indecision, Ray Evart released Polk and gave him a boot toe toward his waiting bronc. Sheathing the gun, he told them: "What I said about paying the doctor bill still stands. But I think you'd better go find him, and not waste any more of your time."

Silently they piled into their battered hulls, Polk looking a bit dazed and as though he were not at all sure what had happened to him. Ray watched them ride away, made sure they took the right turn to reach the doctor's house. Then he leaned for his hat, that had fallen off in the brief scuffle.

There was some blood on his face, and painful bruises where Polk's wild blows had landed. Ray used a bandanna on them, gingerly. After that he stepped to the hitch pole and jerked loose the reins of his gelding.

Dusk was thick in the main street, and in the Valley's bowl beyond the town. A few lights had come on, but otherwise Fowler lay still and lifeless. Ray was glad that this was so, and that the scene there at the sidewalk's edge had caused little disturbance, attracted little attention. The folly of the men from Squatter Town could have set blood flowing in the dust of the street.

He shrugged, and swinging to saddle put his tired bronc on the trail to the Question Mark.

His own weariness, and the day's happenings, rode heavily on him. He thought again of Tim Riley, of the last sickening blow that had laid the spunky Irishman flat with a broken jaw. Well, Ray decided, he had learned one thing today in any event. It had been brought home to him that size and weight, paired with a too ready pugnacity, could make a dangerous force that must be curbed; and the thought of Riley, and of the scorn in the eyes of a squatter's girl, shamed him but sobered him too.

Chapter Six

The Question Mark was a bunching of light and lazy sound in the full quiet dark of evening, when Ray dropped down toward it an hour later. He saw the lampglow streaming from the open windows and doors of the bunkhouse and from the cookshack and barn and other outbuildings, in the normal bustle and activity at the tail end of a busy day. The main house itself was still dark, except for a shaded lamp in the living room and the square of light that marked old Bob's study window.

At the corral below the barn Ray swung down tiredly, stripped saddle and bridle from his gelding and turned the weary bronc into the pen. He slung the heavy stock saddle across the top pole, smoothed the sweaty blanket carefully so it would not wrinkle as it dried. Then he walked up toward the house.

By the bunkhouse door a group of punchers were gathered for a smoke in the quiet dusk; their voices trailed off suddenly as Ray approached. Jack Dalley straightened quickly, and took his spurred boot down from where he had it cocked up behind him, against the wall.

Ray nodded to them all, and spoke a quiet greeting that they answered in a straggle of voices. To one of them Evart said, "Would you take a look at my bronc, Barney? He's been exercising this afternoon and could maybe do with a rubdown. I got business with Bob right now."

The youngster nodded, said, "Sure." Somehow, Ray felt a reserve in the men that amounted almost to lack of respect. This was new, and he was puzzled by it. Perhaps some echo of his quarrel with Bob Craig had reached the men, and wrought this change in them.

Then he exchanged a look with Dalley, and it was as though he had never really seen the man before. Something prompted Evart to feel him out with a carelessly intoned, "Evening, Jack."

Thus directly addressed, Dalley had to answer; but he acted as though he would rather not. There was a perceptible pause before he nodded curtly and answered, "Yeah—evening!"

Ray went on to the big house, a vague irritation riding him. It faded at once into the background as he caught sight of Janet Craig in the half-light of the deep veranda.

Will Ormsby was with her. That was hardly surprising. He had barely taken time to get the travel stains removed and his riding clothes

changed to something more respectable, before
hitting the trail to the Question Mark and Bob
Craig's brown-haired girl; and Ray Evart couldn't
say that he blamed him.

It was the only point on which he knew any
prodding of jealousy, of Ormsby or any other man.
Bob Craig paid good wages, but even a top hand
rider could hardly afford to dream. No, a man had
to own his own brand; and though a deep and real
friendship existed between Janet Craig and her
father's foreman, it hardly seemed likely that, in
the nature of things, it could ever amount to more.

As he came up the steps now Janet met him; her
smile of greeting faded a little as the lamp behind
the window laid its faint sheen across the planes
of his face. She exclaimed, "Why, Ray! What—?"

Evart shrugged, reaching to touch the swollen
cut that Polk's knuckles had put across his forehead. "It isn't anything," he said. He looked at
Will Ormsby, saw the Box O rancher's quizzical
glance. Two fights in one afternoon! he thought to
himself—not a flattering picture. Ormsby's amused
smile had justification, all right, but it irritated
him. He said shortly, "Evening, Will."

Still seated, Ormsby nodded. The girl's hand
laid on his arm brought Evart's attention back to
her, and she was saying, "I've been waiting for
a chance to talk to you, Ray, about—about every-

thing. It's been terrible in the Valley, these last days. I respect your judgment, and I want to know what you think of it all."

Ray shook his head. "My opinion isn't worth too much, Jan. After all," he reminded her, "I've been away too, like Will and your father. I haven't really got into the feel of things here in Donover. But if you really want to know—I think that someone has been playing both ends against the middle!"

Janet stared at him, perplexed, and Ormsby sat forward sharply in his chair. It was Will who said, "How do you mean, Evart?"

Looking at them both, Ray shook his head again. "It's something that I'm not very clear about myself yet. I'm even sorry I brought it up—and if it's all right I'd like to let it drop until I've spoken to Bob."

"You're talking in riddles," Janet accused him. "But Dad's in his office, if you want him. At least I think he is. I haven't seen him myself yet; I wasn't here when he got in, and he went and shut himself away and hasn't once come out. I can see the light under the door, though I knocked once or twice and he didn't answer."

"That's strange," Evart muttered, frowning. "He was pretty sour with me today, though. This thing has really got him."

Will Ormsby rose, and came to join them. "Maybe you haven't heard, Ray," he remarked soberly. "The Question Mark has moved across the river."

"*What!*"

A sense of cold disaster crept through Ray Evart as Ormsby related briefly what he had been able to learn from Craig's riders. It explained the change of the crew's attitude toward him, and Jack Dalley's open insolence. But more than that, it showed the complete lack of realism with which old Bob had attacked the crisis in Donover.

"He's all kinds of an idiot!" Ray fumed, as Will concluded. He glanced quickly at Janet, then added: "I shouldn't say that, but it's the truth. He's playing right into the hands of someone who is a hundred times smarter and craftier, and who laid the bait knowing Bob would rise to it. And he'll have this range steeped in blood before he's finished!"

"You're talking in riddles again," Jan told him. "What are you hinting at? What do you mean by 'someone'? Wasn't it those people from Squatter Town who began this trouble?"

Ray shook his head wearily. "You should know better than that, Jan. You've heard their side of it—about the raid on Chet Black's homestead. That was the real start of it."

"I see what you mean," Will Ormsby put in, frowning as though working with a sudden new thought and its possible meanings. "We've all been assuming that it was one of the ranchers who ordered that done, and then wasn't willing to own up to it. But what if we should be wrong?"

"And now Bob Craig has thrown the fat in the fire!" Ray finished bitterly. He turned suddenly to the door. "He needs a talking to. He's got to be made to see what he's done."

His hand was on the knob when Janet stopped him. She came hardly to big Ray Evart's shoulder; and the brown curls fell back from her face as she tipped it up to him and showed, in the light from the window, the concern written in her soft features. "Ray!" she cautioned him. "Please—you know you've quarreled with him once today. I—I'm afraid!"

He looked down at her in cold amazement. "Afraid of what?"

"Oh, you wouldn't understand!" she cried, bitter exasperation in her voice. "It's just that—that you both have awful tempers. You know it's true."

"No, I guess I don't understand," he admitted angrily. "I just know your dad's gone too far this time—and I've got to pound some sense into that stubborn hide of his if I kill him doing it!"

And he left her standing there, and slammed

the door behind him. Down the long hall, at the far back of the house, a pencil of light across the floor marked the door of Bob's room. Ray strode back and rapped at the closed panels sharply. "It's Evart, Bob. I got to talk to you!"

There was no answer. He waited, knocked again; and then, when Bob Craig still refused to open the door or even speak to him, Ray deliberately dropped a big knuckled hand on the knob and twisted it.

The opening of the door sucked a draft through the window, making the lamp flicker and stirring papers on the desk's scarred top; but old Bob was not in his chair behind the desk and for a moment Ray thought the room was empty. Then his glance dropped to the shadows of the floor, and, horrified, he stared at Bob Craig's silent form. In that first glance, he recognized the familiar paper knife which some hand had taken from its place on the desk, and plunged into Bob Craig's back, between the shoulders.

Ray's first thought was of Janet. It made him close the door carefully, so that she should not come in unexpectedly and see her father's murdered body. Then he went over to the desk and onto one knee at Bob Craig's side.

Bob had not bled much, except internally; a thin crimson trickle marked the ugly wound, and the knife still in it. Ray dazedly touched the silver handle thinking to draw it out, but then reconsidered. The law would not want that.

It was a case for the law, of course. For once Joe Buckley would have to drag his lazy carcass out from the county seat, and give himself some bother over the affairs of Donover. In a welter of thoughts, Ray found himself wondering what new elements this crime would add to the dim confusion in the Valley.

But just then Bob Craig moaned feebly. Quickly Ray turned him over, so that the silvered head lolled back against his arm. No, Bob was not quite dead. A feeble effort still kept some spark of life flickering in him, and now with the last of his strength he was saying something to Ray Evart—something that came out only as a frightful bubbling because of the blood that was in his throat and in his lungs. Bending over him, straining to hear, Ray could make out only a word or two. Something that sounded like *"drawer."*

The whispered voice broke off, its message lost. The mighty effort of speaking had drained the life that still remained in old Bob Craig. In a daze, Ray Evart realized that the old man was dead.

What had Bob been trying to say to him? He looked over at the desk, with its flickering lamp and littered top. Bob had been sitting there when the blow had struck, his back to the murderer. Then, to judge from the position of the chair, rolled back from it, he had tried to come to his feet and had slumped sideward, full length.

Drawer . . .

The desk had three of them on each side. On an impulse Ray Evart began pulling them open, one after the other, in search of some nameless thing. The drawers bristled with a wild clutter of papers, crammed so full—in old Bob's untidy way—that it took an effort to force them open. Ray tried riffling through their contents haphazardly, on the chance that he might uncover something important enough for the old man to have spoken of it with his dying breath. But the aimless search went unrewarded. It would have taken a careful examination of each paper in turn to tell whether any had importance; most were old bills, letters, circulars, stock notices.

Ray pushed the last drawer shut finally and straightened, standing alone there in the utter quiet of the room, trying to think. Idly, his fingers gathered the papers the window's draft had scattered across the desk top, putting them in order; and in so doing he uncovered a block of scratch paper.

It caught and held his quick attention. For a

name stared up at him from the top of the pad—
scrawled over and over, in old Bob's hand, covering the page: the one word, "Duncan."

Sounds of footsteps in the hall jerked him to
awareness. He had forgotten the passage of time
in his futile search of the desk. Now someone
was coming, and he remembered Jan.

He met her outside the door, his big frame blocking the way. "Don't go in there!" he told her, and
put both hands gently on her slender shoulders.
"You mustn't!"

She stared at him, her brown eyes wide with
apprehension. "What—what is it?" she demanded.

Will Ormsby came up behind her. Over the girl's
head Ray met his eye and jerked his head toward
the office; Will hesitated, looking startled, then
quickly edged past them and through the door.

"Ray!" Jan's voice was stifled. "Answer me! I
—I want to know what's happened in there!"

He told her quietly, "Your father's dead, Jan."
And saw her draw away from him with horror in
her eyes.

"And you—you said you would make him see
things your way if you had to kill him doing it!"

It was his turn to stare. For a moment he could
not believe that she was serious, until he read
the look in her eyes. "Good God!" he exclaimed.
"You can't really think—"

But when he stepped toward her she backed off from him as though he were some poisonous thing.

Will Ormsby appeared at the door of the office again, halted with one hand gripping the jamb, white-knuckled, as he looked from Ray to the horrified girl. Evart turned to him wearily. "It's the shock," he said. "Take her into the living room, Will, and see if you can make her lie down. I'll try to get the doc out here."

It was a big, dark living room, with its old-fashioned furniture and the bric-a-brac Jan's mother had brought with her to Donover so many years before. After Ray had dispatched a rider to town, he went in and found the girl stretched out on the couch staring at nothing. Will Ormsby turned distractedly. "She won't answer me," he said. "Won't even look at me!"

"Best let her alone," Ray suggested in a voice that sounded flat in his own ears. "She'll come around when the first shock passes."

Will ran a hand through dark hair that had slight touches of gray about the temples. "Tell me," he demanded. "What did happen in the office?"

The Question Mark ramrod gave him the brief facts, tersely; and as he finished a sound from the archway made them turn and they saw that Jack Dalley had been standing there, listening.

"Dead?" Jack echoed, his full face showing an astonishment that bordered on disbelief. He came into the room, looking at the other two men.

Will nodded. "What you just heard Evart tell about it is all any of us know."

Young Dalley's expression changed suddenly. "I'm not so sure about that," he answered flatly. His glance came to bear on Evart, and it had a sharp suspicion in it. "Seems to me he's got a lot more explaining to do!"

Ray's face went hard. "Yes?"

"I wasn't eavesdropping, Evart, but I couldn't help hearing what you said to Miss Craig out there on the porch just before you went into the office—you were all talking loud, and voices carry at night. You said you'd kill him! And next thing, they found you alone and Craig was dying!"

Will lifted a hand, looking shocked. "Wait a minute, Dalley. That's harsh talk."

Ray motioned Ormsby to silence. "Let him finish!" he said tightly. "Go on, Jack. And so you think I murdered Bob?"

Dalley shrugged his shoulders uneasily. "I don't say that for sure. I just say we better get the sheriff in here; and when he does come, there'll be some questions he might want you to answer—"

"Go on!" Ray repeated, his cold eyes level. "Just why do you think I killed Craig?"

"Because, damn it, you were mad!" Dalley exploded suddenly. "Because I figure you stormed in to give him a piece of your mind—and he told you you were fired."

Will Ormsby said: "That's nonsense!"

"Yes? Ask Sol Bingham—he was with me this evening when Craig said he couldn't get along with Evart any more and that I was to be the new foreman of the Question Mark. Or ask any of the hands—they all knew it. Craig was just waiting for you to show up so he could give you your time. And I'll bet money you went in a rage right then and there and—"

"It's a lie!" Ray Evart gritted, and would have waded in on Dalley if Will had not stopped him. After that his temper subsided and he got a grip on himself again, with a quick anger at his own lack of self-control.

Will Ormsby was saying, "For God's sake, let's stay cool about this. Part of what Jack says could be true, Ray—I mean about Bob's firing you. Remember, he threatened to—out on the range; and when he made up his mind to push across the river he must have known that you would never go along with him on such a play. He may have decided right then that he'd have to make a change."

Ray could only nod shortly to that; for the truth

of it struck him hard. And then Will went on: "As for the rest, I think Jack's making a bad guess there. I know you too well, Ray! Moreover, there would have been an argument first—and I have a notion we could have heard that from out on the porch, even with the office door closed. But we didn't hear a sound!"

Jack Dalley still looked skeptical, unconvinced. "I dunno," he said. "There's a city jail in Fowler. As Bob Craig's foreman, I say this guy ought to be taken in and put there until the sheriff's had a chance at him."

Ray's fists curled, opened again. "You care to try doing it?"

The younger man's look touched Evart's, wavered a little under it. He said sullenly, "Not by myself."

Ray let the tightness out of his body. "All right," he said. "Just so we know where we stand. But two things I want you to remember, Jack, until this is straightened out. First: It's Miss Jan's ranch now, and what she wants is what's going to be done here. And secondly: I don't know how long either or both of us is going to be around— but while we are, you had better stay pretty clear of me. Understand?"

Chapter Seven

Dawn brought a mist from the river, gray streamers that hung and twisted among the buildings and bunched in tamarisk branches before the Question Mark's main house; its low veil hid the snowcap Valley rim. Ray's saddle blanket was still damp and sour. He got another, and threw a hull across the back of a big-barreled gray. Morning's bleak chill bit into him as he jerked up the cinches.

Leading his mount across the ranch yard, he met some of the punchers straggling out from breakfast. Sight of him chopped their talk off like a knife blade, and he felt the hostility in their looks and steeled himself against it.

"Morning," he said briefly; but no one answered him and Ray went on. Jack Dalley had been talking to them. Ray could see already that, in the eyes of the men, he stood all but convicted of the crime that had struck the Question Mark.

Made sombre by this thought, he reached the house and left his bronc, to step inside a moment. Doc MacGowan was sitting sleepily on the edge of the living room sofa, rumpling white hair and yawning; the blanket and pillow he had thrown aside made a heap on the floor near his shoes, which were the only part of his clothing he had taken off before turning in. Yesterday had been a busy day for him.

He nodded shortly to Ray. Evart asked, "How is Miss Craig?"

"Oh, she'll be all right. She was sleeping like a lamb when I left her. We'd better not disturb her until she wakes of her own accord. Rest and plenty of it is what she needs."

"Will you be going back to town this morning?"

The doctor said, "Yes, I'd better. Maybe I can come out again later in the day."

"All right. The cook will fix you up with breakfast."

Ray Evart went again to the office, where Bob Craig's body still lay on the floor with a sheet covering it. He stood looking at the vague form a moment, and then stepped to the desk. Someone had made an attempt at tidying the mess in which Bob and the wind had left it. The papers were piled neatly under paper weights; and he saw that the top sheet of the pad with its repeated name, "Duncan," had been ripped off and disposed of.

Going out, he paused at the door of Jan's room and caught the quiet sound of her steady breathing, in sleep. As he listened he thought again of the previous night and the terrible thing she had said to him. He wanted to talk to her, now that the shock had been eased by slumber, and to see if her eyes would still hold the accusation that had been there.

Surely, in the light of day and calmer reason, she would know that he could not have killed her father. And yet Ray felt a reluctance to face her —a dread of finding her doubt of him still in her eyes.

In any event she was asleep now and he could not disturb her. He returned to his waiting bronc, before the house, and lifted into saddle.

There were scurrying clouds low above the river mist, and the damp chill clung to everything.

Ray Evart quartered across the Question Mark range, letting the gray have its head; the bronc bucked a little at first, kicking life into its limbs and muscles, but then he got it quiet and it settled down into a long lope that ate up the morning miles. Engrossed as he was in his own thoughts, Ray reached the mist-crowned river before he realized. It slipped silently between its banks, somehow eerie in the half-light of morning. The icy water was a shock against his legs as he put the gray into it.

He came up the other bank onto enemy ground.

A mile or so beyond Ray Evart reined up, finally, and leaned forward slightly with palms crossed upon the saddle horn. He had wanted to see with his own eyes Question Mark beef on nester ground; and here it was.

The cattle were grazing quietly, weaving a slow pattern of red and white across the green earth. Yonder, Ray saw the clutter of stones and charred beam ends that had been a farmer's cabin, before the torch had taken it. And now one of Bob Craig's riders was coming toward him, stepping his pony gingerly over the twisted strands of a cut and leveled fence.

"Better clean that out," Ray told him, indicating the sharp-fanged wire. "It could cripple the stock, if they got into it."

"I was goin' to," the other answered shortly.

More of Jack Dalley's work. Ray considered the man with a slow, critical appraisal, but chose not to take issue with him. After all, like the other riders, this one no longer considered Evart his boss; and moreover half suspected him of murdering old Bob.

Ray held himself in check now, though something hot burned in him at the open challenge of the man's look and tone. The issue would be straightened out when Jan Craig decided for herself who was to be her foreman; and though he

privately feared it would be Jack Dalley, there
seemed little he could do about it.

So, ignoring the tone of the man's curt answer,
he asked: "Has there been any kind of trouble
—with the nesters, I mean?"

The man shrugged. "Naw. Three of them rode
by an hour ago."

"What did they do?"

"Nothing. Kept their distance; looked over the
layout, and went away again. Yeah," he added,
with a short laugh, "they know they got company,
all right. But they ain't come to call!"

Ray frowned. "You needn't laugh," he grunted.
"They'll be here sooner or later."

"I reckon we can give 'em a warm welcome,"
the man countered, and spat.

Evart studied him a moment. "I don't suppose
it would do any good for me to order you and the
boys to move these critters back across the river,
where they belong?"

"Not a bit of good," came the bland reply.
"You're wasting your time, Evart. Nobody on
this payroll takes orders from you any longer. I
don't see why you even hang around—after what
you did last night!"

It cost Evart a struggle with himself, but he
did not rise to that bait. Slowly, painfully, he
was learning some of the self-control whose lack

had shown him in a bad light more than once already. He only met the cowhand's taunt with a slow, steady look that made the other twist a little, uncomfortably. When his anger was firmly controlled, Ray said quietly:

"We'll just skip that, for now. Meanwhile, better keep your eyes open if you value your skin. The nesters might not let you have the first shot!"

He left that thought for the rider to chew on, and turned back to the river.

Presently he could hear the whisper of it slipping between willow-hung banks; the mist drifting thickly. Trees stood out, showing dimly. Evart reined in at another sound, and sat waiting as a pair of horses took form and bulked through the rising gray streamers.

He knew Jack Dalley's black before he recognized the rider. The man with him, Ray saw then, was Sheriff Joe Buckley.

At that same moment they recognized him, and the way their broncs fought the reins showed how nervously the pair jerked up. It gave Evart warning. His face held no expression as he met their gaze, but there was a tension all through him.

"Morning, Joe," he greeted the sheriff. "You're out early."

Buckley was an ineffectual man, with faded eyes and beard. He held his riding bronc constantly under tight rein, so that the poor animal had long ago been ruined by the torture of the bit. The sheriff had his coat buttoned high now but it did not protect him from the dank chill; spasms of shivering ran through his thin frame as he sat saddle next to Dalley. "I heard the news," he said. "About Craig, I mean—a rider brought it in last night, and I came right over."

"Glad you did." Ray studied the sheriff's weak face. "You've heard about the other, too—about what happened here day before yesterday? Maybe," he suggested, "you ought to have come a little sooner."

Joe Buckley let his breath out sharply, and it made a streamer of gray in front of his face. Jack Dalley cut in: "Evart, don't talk to the law that way!"

Ray shrugged. The sheriff had his breath back now and he hunched forward a little in the big coat, his face twisted with resentment. "That wasn't a very wise remark—not from you!" he snapped. "Jack told me about last night—and what passed between you and Craig before they found you alone with his body. That's the reason we rode out this way together. We were looking for you!"

"Yes?" Ray said the word very quietly. "Well, you've seen me; what about it?"

"I want you to come into town with me," Buckley said. "For questioning. We're going to dig into this."

Looking from one to the other of them, Ray Evart read their temper. Alone, Joe Buckley was not much to handle; but he had Dalley's backing and Dalley was ambitious. Jack, he knew, had become a potential source of danger. It would not be wise to give that young man too great an opportunity.

That made up Ray's mind. "I'm not coming," he said. He made it a simple statement of fact; but the gunmetal that came into his fingers at the same moment put teeth into it.

They gaped at him and at the unexpected draw, and Buckley's skittish horse crab-walked as the sheriff jerked reins convulsively. Then Jack Dalley started swearing. Ray told him: "That isn't necessary, Jack. I've just decided I don't want to let you put me out of the way—not at a moment like this. I didn't kill Bob; I don't know who did. But I do know that I can't afford to go to jail—not even for a day or two—with things the shape they are in this Valley. Sorry to disappoint you."

Buckley's voice came out with an effort, but his hands stayed safely clear of the walnut-butted gun in his own holster. "Evart, you'll never get anywhere defying the law! It's my job to see that it's respected—and I know my duty."

"Respect for the law has been a pretty scarce article here in Donover, for the last three days," Ray pointed out bluntly. "If you had been here then, the killing of Bob Craig might have been avoided. I don't say for sure it would, but it might have been. There's more behind all this than you have any idea, Joe. For one thing, I happen to know for a fact that Sid Roberts is tangled up in it."

"Roberts?" The sheriff snorted. "That's fantastic! You'll never make me believe anything like that."

"I thought not," Ray answered drily. "Which is why I'm not going to waste my time trying to convince you, or pound sense into your skull. Now, both of you," he added crisply, "unsling your guns and pass them over—careful!"

They did not want to, but they had let Evart surprise them and now there was no help for it. With open reluctance, Jack Dalley unbuckled his cartridge belt, looped it around the scarred holster, and handed it to Ray. His smooth round face had a sullen look in it as he did so; bristling anger showed weakly in Joe Buckley as the latter followed suit.

After he had both their guns, Ray Evart returned his own to its sheath but kept his hand on it. "I'll leave these for you up the way a little," he told them. "I just didn't like the idea of you taking shots at me when I rode off."

"What do you think you're going to do?" the sheriff demanded.

"Find out who killed Bob Craig," Ray answered. "And what is the meaning of the trouble in Donover Valley. I couldn't do that in jail."

"You'll *be* in jail, if I get another chance at you! After this, I'm out to get you, Evart. Remember that!"

Jack Dalley grumbled sharply: "Oh, let him go! We muffed our chance, and talking's no good now!"

Evart touched the gray with his knees, drew away from the pair and then turned his bronc along the misty river bank. He went away from there at a canter—not hurrying, but without giving them too much time either to think the thing over before he was well gone.

A quarter mile farther on he reined in beside a cottonwood and leaned to drape the gun belts that he had taken across a prominent lower limb. If Jack and the sheriff wanted to come after them they could get them. After that he put his bronc into a faster gait, to put distance between him and that spot.

He rode south, keeping the steaming river at

his right until it began its broad curve in upon itself. Then he crossed and went up to higher ground beyond, on the cowmen's side.

Looking down into the crook of the river's arm, he could see from there the nester settlement on its muddy bank. Smoke from stovepipes pencilled the dull morning sky; the people there had begun their early business of the day. Ray thought of the Irishman, Tim Riley, and of that nester girl who had told him off the day before. The doctor had said that Riley was not in bad condition from his smashed jaw, and that weighed easier on Evart's conscience. He would have liked to talk to those people now; but he decided against trying it.

Ahead of him, the bleak broken rim of the southern wall cut a jagged edge along the sky. His business lay yonder.

He struck out across the rolling bottom lands, and finally the foothills lifted under him. Hours passed as he climbed up toward the barren rim; it was noon when he came out of the timber of the hills, and glancing down saw the river like a leaden streak under the threatening sky. After that he rode with caution, for he was nearing the scene of yesterday's gunbattle, below the face of the notched cliff. There again was the cleft, and the boulder behind which he had taken cover.

He saw at once that the body of the dead bandit, Legg, had been removed.

Ray Evart considered the thing from a little distance, letting his gray blow after its stiff climb. The ever present wind blew strongly down at him through the cleft, with a roar and a steady whipping at his sombrero. If there was any other sound, the wind covered it. After a long survey Ray Evart spoke to his bronc and sent it up the steep slope of talus, up toward the shadowed throat of the notch.

Nothing stirred. Eyes alert, hand on gun, Ray Evart pushed on into the narrow break of the rimrock wall.

Chapter Eight

It extended for three hundred yards or so, splitting native rock of a hardness that had resisted for centuries the further work of wind and weather. There was no sign of the horsemen Ray knew had ridden through the notch. His own gray struck sparks with iron shoes, but it left no prints on the rock-ribbed floor.

He came up to the other mouth of the cleft, at the farther side of the huge upthrust; and saw the high country stretched out in a shallow hogback, cut with spurs and breaking miles beyond in a mass of tumbled badlands. Here the winds swept constantly, beating particles of rock into Evart's squinted eyes. Scrub growth clung to the bleak rocks, with scattered stands of timber lower down. The thickening clouds scudded low above the peaks. It would be storming before many hours, in this high malpais.

It was unfamiliar ground to Ray Evart; no Valley business had ever before brought him up to this trackless and forgotten region. He sat braced for a long time against the beat of the streaming wind, studying the shape of the land.

Then he directed his attention to the slope that dropped away immediately before him.

He began circling, breaking for sign. He struck it finally—what practically amounted to a trail made by shod hoofs where enough soil clung to the rimrock to take an imprint. Legg had come this way, and the other man he had encountered in battle the afternoon before. Perhaps, also, the elusive stranger whose appearance so puzzled him.

The trail took Evart down into the maze of spurs and scrub growth, away from the notch. The wind rode with him, pushing against him like a hand, spurting grit and dust around him. It was after noon, but the clouds lay low and thick enough to absorb much of the day's light. In the half-gloom, scrub cedar clung grimly to barren rock, holding against the wind that rattled in leafless branches.

After a mile or so, he found he had lost the trail again in the harder rock of a deep gully, and pulled up there, considering. As he did so a drop of rain splattered sharply against his cheek. Ray glanced at the low ceiling; blue sky showed among the hurrying rags of cloud, but the storm was coming.

He dismounted. The gray would stand to trailing reins; Evart left him that way and worked on afoot, up the steep slope of the wash to its scrub-crested top. He approached the ridge cautiously; beyond, a better view of the country below opened up to him.

Rolling hills and hollows, blue with pine growth, showed. Ray Evart studied this scene carefully, mile on mile. Suddenly then he brought his glance back again to something he had nearly passed over.

Distance and cloud haze obscured the view. Still, he could make out the shape of a brush-cleared hollow, under steep walls at three sides; and he could see now the weather-stained buildings that at first glance blended into their background. There were two, mere shanties. They were very old, with no rawness left by the scars of the axe blade. Nearby was what looked like a pole corral, and an open shed or leanto constructed against the rock wall of the box canyon. The movement of horses in the corral indicated its use, and there was also a blue line of smoke that rose from a shack's battered stovepipe.

Ray Evart, flattened against the rocks to avoid skylining himself, studied the scene with satisfaction. It was what he had wanted to find. He judged the distance, figured the route that would take him down in that direction. He slid away from the crest, was about to come to his feet when the rifle slug spatted sharply near him and screamed off toward the gray heavens.

He froze.

The echoes of the shot rolled away, and there was the fresh scar chipped into the rock, only inches from his body; but he could not begin to guess from what direction the bullet had come. He knew he was perfectly exposed there on the bleak rock—an excellent target. Perhaps the rifleman thought that first shot had been better than it was, for long moments dragged out and still no other came.

A small sweat dotted Ray Evart's forehead. He heard the high wind screaming overhead, the rattling of the brush. Below and behind him the gray horse scraped iron against rock, shifting position. But there was nothing else—no other sign of the bushwhacker or of the rifle that might be still trained against his back.

With as little movement as possible, Ray began getting into position. A slight twist of his left arm put the palm against the ground; he shifted his weight there and came up a little onto the balls of his feet, crouching tensed. From a distance he must still give the appearance of sprawling limply where the pound of lead had put him.

He came up quickly, springing nimbly away. The rifle spoke again, at once, but the shot was wild; and now from the corner of his eye Evart caught a glimpse of smoke, filming out on the tail of the shot, and at once his six-gun was in his

hand and he snapped a slug in that direction.
It was really too much range for a short gun—a
spot above him, on a higher ridge at his back. But
the try had been almost an instinctive action on
Evart's part. Off balance as he was, the bucking
of the weapon in his hand kicked him strongly; his
foot slipped, and he went tumbling and crashing
down the short slope.

He lost the six-gun. But when he could get to
his feet again he scrambled up and saw the weapon
where it had slid to a stop not more than a dozen
feet away. He lunged, got it; went on toward his
waiting bronc.

He heard the rifle's whine once more, but far
overhead. The rifleman had lost the range for the
moment. Before he could get it again Evart was
in the saddle and ramming the spurs home. The
gray, a highstrung animal, responded with a bucking leap that all but spilled its rider. After that,
however, Ray's firm hand quieted it and the bronc
straightened out into a gallop away from there.

At the head of the dry wash Evart reined in
for a brief look back the way he had come. Quickly,
he saw his attacker. The man was mounted and
coming downslope after him, bent low over the
neck of his cayuse and with his rifle still in one
hand. Ray Evart touched the stock of the carbine
under his own right knee. At that distance a run-

ning horse would be hard to hit, but even so he thought he could make the shot and drop the rider. He decided against it, however, not wanting to mix in gunplay there; the next moment the pursuer had dropped down into the gully and the chance was gone.

Ray turned again and sent his pony forward.

He skylined a hump, went down the other slope in brush that clawed at him as he flashed through. After that there were rolling hills of pine, and he let the gray pick its own course down through them. His primary aim was to lose the pursuer tailing him; after that, to get closer to the corral and cabins he had seen from above.

But the other horseman knew these hills, and it was proving harder than Ray had imagined to shake him. Minutes sped by; the gray was tiring, and on top of that Evart began to fear becoming lost in unfamiliar territory.

He reined in suddenly, at the steep lip of an old washout that flanked his way. At the foot of the slide thick brush offered a hope of protection. Ray glanced back; quickly put his pony to the drop. The gray protested, but on urging took the slide with forelegs braced; rock dust boiled up, loose gravel sprayed. Then they struck level ground again with a jolt and Evart straightened the bronc out.

But almost at once a break in the gait of the horse warned him something was wrong. After only a dozen strides the gray was limping. Evart cursed, halted the bronc and swung down.

During the slide, a stone had become lodged under the shoe on the bronc's rightforefoot. Evart fished out his pocket knife, thumbed it open, bent and began hastily digging at the stone.

Behind him a voice said: "When you've finished what you're doing, just turn around—real easy!"

Surprised that way, there was nothing Ray could do for himself. Yet he controlled his alarm. With great deliberateness he went ahead and dislodged the stone, set the hoof on the ground. Then he straightened, knife still in hand, and turned slowly to face the man with the gun.

It was no one he remembered ever having seen before. A bearded, shabby figure; only the cartridge belt and oiled holster, and the shining gun in his hand, looked well cared for. "Well, and who are you?" the hoarse voice demanded.

"Nobody you'd know," Ray told him shortly. He was standing with arms half raised, obedient to the black gun muzzle. "How about taking them down?" he suggested.

"Drop the knife, first."

Ray opened his hand, let the little blade fall. Then his captor moved in, giving the knife a kick with his foot, and snaked the six-shooter from his prisoner's holster. He stepped back with it, motioning with the point of his own gun. "Now move away from that bronc, because I don't want you trying to make a jump for it . . . All right. You can put your arms down."

Evart did so, slowly. "What's the deal?" he said.

"I'll ask the questions," the bearded man retorted. "What do you think you're doing up here? Better have a good answer ready."

Instead, Ray Evart shot a sudden look past him; and the other sidestepped into position where he could keep one eye on his prisoner and also cover the back trail. Another horseman had come plowing down the rock slide, rifle in hand, his bronc's muzzle streaming foam. He reined in, exclaiming: "Good! You stopped him for me."

"He came larrupin' down that rock slide, right past me. Who the hell is he, Mort?"

Mort shook his head, steadying his nervous bronc and leaning forward with the rifle across his knee. "Looked like a snooper to me. I took a shot at him a piece back—thought I'd hit him, too, but he was only playing possum. A pretty smart boy, you know it?"

"Get me on the wrong end of the gun next time," Ray told him icily, "and you won't feel too smart yourself—bushwhacker!"

Mort went hard and mean at that. "Better go easy!" he snapped. "It's kind of tough for you right now, and I think it's gonna get tougher!"

"Not really!" Evart came back at him scornfully.

It was not easy playing that role, with both those guns in command. But Evart had his captors pegged as hard men who could only be impressed by a superior hardness. Any sign of fear would be fatal; but as long as he maintained a cool front he could keep some shred of control over the situation.

The bearded man ventured, frowning: "Do you suppose we ought to let the boss see him?"

"Ah!" Ray approved, nodding. "The first intelligent thing I've heard yet. I've come a long way to talk to Sid Roberts!"

The mention of that name had an immediate effect. It washed a look of blank astonishment over the bearded face of the man on the ground, but Mort turned narrow-eyed and suspicious. "What are you talking about? I never heard of no Sid Roberts—"

Evart made a gesture of annoyance. "You aren't even funny. I know he's moved into this rimrock country, and I know you're part of his gang. I also know that was his layout I saw from the ridge, back yonder. Now, stop arguing and take me down there!"

The two exchanged looks. This stranger who wouldn't scare and who had such amazing information was apparently more than they could figure out. Finally Mort shrugged. "Why not?" he grunted. "Get your cayuse, Vic."

It was a rat-tailed nag that Vic led out of the brush where he had tied it. He swung into the scarred, double-rig saddle. Then Mort put his bronc up alongside Evart's gray and leaned to jerk the carbine from the saddle boot. Ray's six-gun was tucked in the bearded man's waistband.

"All right," Mort said briefly. "That pulls your fangs. You can get back on now."

Wordlessly, Ray Evart swung up and the pair ranged their horses on either side of his. He read the alertness in their manner, knew they would be taking no chances and leaving no moment unguarded. For the time being he was very thoroughly a prisoner.

A sudden gust of wind blew hard against them as they started out, flattening hat brims down and making them duck their heads against it. The clouds were scurrying overhead. A handful of raindrops lashed them, fell away. A belt of cold air moved in across the high wastes.

They set a course down the pine-choked hills. Ray Evart had momentarily lost his directions;

but he got squared around again a moment later when the country fell clear before them, suddenly, and the shacks and corral showed only a mile or so away. He studied the layout as they approached. The log shacks had a timeless look about them, and also an appearance of having been patched repeatedly as the original materials wore out. The stovepipes slanted crazily; broken windows were boarded up or plugged with rags. Half a dozen horses stamped in the brush corral, and the leanto beside it showed now as an open shed for storing saddles and equipment, built hard against the rock wall of the cut.

Minutes later they rode into the protection of the box and at once the wind was gone, shut away by its high sides. A man stepped out of a doorway, staring hard at Ray Evart. "Hey!" he exclaimed.

Mort said: "Boss inside?"

The man nodded, clamping his jaw shut on other questions.

At a signal from Mort, Ray Evart lit down in the junk-littered clearing, and Mort joined him with one hand on his gun. "You take the horses," he told Vic shortly. "I'll show this boy inside."

He jerked his head at Ray; and the prisoner followed as Mort pushed open the door of the smaller cabin.

Chapter Nine

It was dismal enough—a single room, dark because of a boarded-up, paneless window, and sparsely filled with makeshift furniture. There was a table, a couple of chairs, a hay-mattress bunk against the wall. An old stove smoked freely.

By a candle stuck into a bottle, a man sat reading at the table. He glanced up irritably as Mort pushed into the room; then his eyes narrowed at sight of the stranger with him. "What's this?" he wanted to know.

"A gent we picked up in the hills, Sid," the other told him. "He won't say what he's after, but—well, he mentioned you by name. Seems to know something. Vic and I thought you ought to talk to him."

Sid Roberts studied the prisoner, fingering the book lying open before him. He was not a big man, but he had a quality that drew attention. His skin, dark as mahogany, was stretched tight over a bony facial structure. A high forehead shone in the candlelight, under a receding hairline. He had a nervous, agile strength.

He said, "What's your name?"

"French." Ray Evart said it levelly, not batting an eye. The outlaw considered the answer a moment.

"Don't think I know you," he observed.

"You don't. But I heard you were down here in this rimrock country, and when things got a little warm for me where I was I took a pasear this way, to look you up."

"Who sent you?"

"No one. I'm on my own."

Roberts lowered heavy brows until they shaded his eyes, pondering. Then he looked up and saw the man called Mort still standing by the door. He shrugged, closed the book—it was *David Copperfield*—and pushed it away from him. To Mort he said, "Leave us alone awhile. I'll talk to him."

The man hesitated. "Think you better?"

Roberts cut him off. "I don't see any guns on him. Go on; leave us alone."

Mort grumbled but went out without further argument, closing the door behind him. Sid Roberts gestured toward the other hide-bottomed chair; while Evart was seating himself Roberts got up, took the book he had been reading and placed it on a narrow shelf on the wall beside the boarded window. There were three or four more volumes on the shelf—a copy of Darwin, Ray noticed among others.

Roberts stretched a little, then took his seat again facing Ray across the table. As he did so his coat gapped open slightly, showing the bulk of a gun in its shoulder holster.

"French," Roberts repeated, musing. "What's your game?"

"Nothing in particular. Anything good that comes up." Ray Evart crossed his knees and made himself comfortable.

"And who told you I had moved in here?"

Evart shook his head. "I'd rather not say," he demurred. "It was sort of roundabout. However— it was let on you had something big on the fire. That's why I came down."

Roberts considered that. He ran a lean palm across his scalp, ruffled the thinning hair and straightened it out again. "Where have you worked?"

"Oh, various places." Ray made an indefinite gesture. "South, quite a bit. Ran some stuff over the border—guns and cattle. Handled some hot ice, too."

"Around Santa Fe?"

Evart hesitated. "Some."

Sid Roberts got a battered pipe from one pocket. From the table at his elbow he took a plug of tobacco and a skinning knife, and began shredding weed into the bowl with quick strokes of his nervous fingers. With all his attention on what his hands were doing, he said, not looking up: "You sound all right, mister, but I still don't know enough about you. Time to find that out later, though . . . As a matter of fact, I do have something good on the fire here."

"Yes?" Ray Evart cast a slow glance around the dirty room. When he tilted his head he could look straight up at the gray sky, through chinks in the roof. He observed drily: "Don't look like so much to me!"

Roberts got his meaning. "This?" he snorted. "Purely temporary! These cabins have been here some ten, fifteen years—left over from the old days; we found we could use them and moved in. We won't be here long."

"I shouldn't think you'd like it much." Ray considered the shelf of books behind the outlaw's shoulder. "A man of your tastes, Roberts, must get fed up sometimes with this kind of life, and the men you have to deal with. Me, I wouldn't care; any place a man hangs his hat's OK. But there's not much for you, holed up like this in the rimrock, is there?"

Roberts had his pipe lighted now. "You got eyes in your head, all right," he admitted. He hunkered down in his chair, and pointed the smoking stem at Evart. "I'm playing for big stakes this time, French—the biggest yet. No, not money; I've got all of that I need, and salted away where I can reach it. But all the cash in the world won't buy the things I want, here in the rimrock."

Ray Evart waited, wondering how much this outlaw chief was going to tell him. But Roberts had lapsed into silence, building clouds of tobacco smoke about his bald and shining brow.

Then, suddenly, he was talking again. "Just over that rim five miles above is the prettiest valley in these northern ranges. Donover—you've maybe heard of it. Rancher by the name of Craig has been running the place ever since anybody can remember, but a few years back he let the nesters in and after that his control started going to pieces. Well, a friend of mine is building now to take over —with my help—and when he does I'll move down there in style. They've even got a town in the Valley; no more rimrock hideout for Sid Roberts! And I'll have the money I've saved, and protection from interference by the county seat. I can retire on that!"

In the outlaw's eyes as he finished was the keen glow of anticipation. He had so built himself up with his own words that he was leaning a little forward in his chair; now he had to let the tension run out of him again, and as he sat back, sucking on the pipe stem, he ran a look of disgust around the shanty, comparing it already, in his mind, with the better scenes that were coming.

Ray Evart waited until he was very sure of himself before he spoke again. "This—friend of yours," he suggested then, cautiously. "Are you certain you can trust him?"

The outlaw grunted, and spat on the littered floor. "I don't trust anybody. Don't get the idea I trust you, either," he added quickly, putting the weight of his sharp glance on Evart, "just because I feel like talking a little free. I could see to it you don't repeat any of this!"

That sounded like a threat, but Evart showed no change of expression.

"Same thing goes for Duncan," Roberts went on. "His hands aren't too clean. I'll queer everything for him if he tries to cut me out. And he knows it!"

Duncan! The name again—the name that fit no person in the Valley. And there was that other matter of the stranger who had spied on the ranchers and led Evart into gun battle with Roberts' men, up near the rimrock cleft. He wondered if Roberts could have told him that stranger's connection with the Valley's reign of terror—and perhaps with the murder of Craig. But it was not a question he could ask.

One other idea suggested itself to him. He said, "What about this old-timer you mentioned—this rancher who used to run Donover? Aren't you going to have trouble with him?"

Roberts shook his head disdainfully. "Craig? Not a bit. He'll play right into our hands. He hates the nesters. By working on the hatred of both sides, we can let the ranchers and the nesters slug it out, and step in later to pick up the pieces."

Evart looked impressed. What really interested him was the indication, from the outlaw's words, that Sid Roberts did not yet know of the murder of Bob Craig and so had had no hand in planning it. That fact might prove valuable later.

Now he asked: "Suppose a free-lancer were to cut himself into this deal. What might there be in it for him?"

"Meaning you?"

Ray nodded.

Sid Roberts dragged at his pipe. "I said before that I don't know you, mister. I'd as soon gut-shoot you and leave you for the buzzards as waste a minute on you!"

Evart smiled thinly, though he did not feel like smiling. "I don't think you'll do that," he murmured.

"No?" A cross-current had built up between them suddenly. Ray Evart met the bright, hard look of the outlaw, and tried to better it; wished he could read the thoughts behind that dark forehead. The scene ended abruptly as a hand fell on the latch of the door and the man named Mort stuck his head into the room.

"Sid!" the man exclaimed. "Sorry to interrupt, but we got another one out here. Just rode in. He's from Duncan!"

"Duncan?" Roberts was on his feet at once. "Anything wrong?"

"I dunno," Mort answered. "This fellow just says he was sent up to make talk. What'll I do with him?"

Roberts shot a sharp glance at Evart. "I'll be right out."

Mort hurried away, leaving the door open. Sid Roberts put out his candle and followed, turning in the doorway for a brief warning. "I wouldn't try to leave if I were you. You wouldn't go far."

Ray shrugged. "Why should I go anywhere? I just got here."

The outlaw turned sharply, slamming the flimsy door. At once Ray Evart was out of his chair. There were two windows in the shack, but only one—that which gave on the wrong side of the building—let in any light. The other, long since broken, had been boarded on the outside and stuffed with rags.

Ray Evart set to work at that window now with cautious fingers, drawing out the dirty cloth and opening a crack through which the light came faintly. He tested it, but could see nothing but brush and sky. One of the boards proved to be loose at one end, however, and by displacing it slightly he succeeded in widening his field of vision.

Now he had a view of the clearing, and the leanto, but not of the brush corral. What was more important, he saw the door of the other shack quite clearly. Sid Roberts and another man were just then entering; Evart had only a glimpse of the latter, not enough to recognize him.

Now Mort made to follow at Roberts' heels, but the outlaw turned and stopped him. Ray saw a word passed between them, saw their eyes move in his direction. When Mort nodded and, instead of going into the room, took a position in the open doorway with arms crossed and one heel cocked up behind him, Evart knew quite plainly that he was a prisoner there, and that Mort would guarantee that he did not leave.

After a moment Ray Evart moved away from the window, convinced that he could see nothing of that conference in the other shanty. As he stood alone in the half-gloom and windy silence, the rain which had so long threatened suddenly came crashing down.

It pounded at the roof, lashed at flimsy walls with the wind behind it. A steady dripping began through the many holes of the cabin's ceiling.

Listening to it, Ray Evart considered his position. He had misplayed his hand in getting himself captured by Roberts' men; though he had used the opportunity to gain knowledge that threw much light on some of the things that puzzled him. There were still so many others, however, that he did not know.

And there remained the prime fact of his present peril. He could not carry on this part indefinitely. The showdown would come—soon—and when it did he would be one against them all, and without a weapon.

That thought sent him prowling through the musty room, examining it more carefully. If he had thought to find a gun among Roberts' possessions, he was disappointed. Finally, pausing at the table where the rain, dripping from the roof, had already formed a puddle on the splintered top, he caught sight of the skinning knife Roberts had forgotten and snatched it up. He put it under his waistband inside the shirt, leaving the shirt unbuttoned.

Through the pounding of the rain he heard voices, then, and hurried back to his window. The conference was over. Sid Roberts came stepping out of the door of the other shanty, hunkering into the coat that he pulled up about his neck. Then, with a sharp intake of breath, Evart caught his first good sight of the man who was with him.

Jack Dalley!

Chapter Ten

In astonishment, Ray Evart squinted through the broken window at Sid Roberts and his visitor, and wondered what he was supposed to deduce from this. It left him as deeply in the dark as ever. The knowledge that Jack Dalley was involved only complicated matters, without giving him any intelligible clue.

Of course, he knew that Jack was caught in the grip of a burning ambition; anything might serve as fuel for that fire. And in the setup Sid Roberts and the mysterious Duncan were planning, there should be great opportunity for a bright young lad of Dalley's tastes and abilities. But it threw the question of Duncan back into Evart's lap. Who could he be, that Jack would serve him?

Someone in the Valley— A renegade rancher, perhaps? Ray ran them over in his mind briefly, without arriving anywhere. Some of the ranchers, he remembered, had suffered already from the night raids of Roberts' crew. Will Ormsby, for example. Ray recalled the shock and anger that had showed in Will's face last evening, when he returned from his trip outside to find a dozen good head of stock wantonly slaughtered. Will certainly hadn't been playing a part then; that emotion had been real.

If not a rancher, Duncan could still be almost anyone else—anyone Roberts would have described as "in solid" with the cattlemen. And there were other facets of the mystery— The unknown rider who had eluded him. And the murder of old Bob.

Ray Evart shook his head, turning away from the window. Dalley was already gone, someone having brought his horse for him. Roberts still stood in the shelter of the other doorway, talking with his men. There were more in camp than Ray had imagined—a half dozen at least that he could count. And some of those were running for horses, setting out in the heavy rain.

He was back in his rawhide-bottomed chair when Sid Roberts' hand fell on the latch. Roberts strode in, leaving the door open; the outlaw showed great excitement, and instead of returning to his own seat he paced over to the table, perching nervously on one corner of it while his keen bright eyes ate into Evart's face.

Ray said nothing, waiting. Outside, the rain, past its first hard torrent, had settled to a steady patter beyond the open door; the damp coolness of it swept into the murky room.

"This is it!" Roberts said suddenly. "We're moving down on Donover! Old Craig was killed last night, and Duncan has sent word he thinks the time is ripe to strike at the nesters and wipe them out. But I'm changing that! I'm making the whole play tonight—cleaning out all the Valley at one stroke before anyone is ready to try and stop us."

Evart said calmly, "A big order, isn't it?"

"Yes. But they're not organized—and we are. Surprise will be our best weapon. But," he added, frowning, "I need every gun I can get. That's why I'd almost be tempted to take a chance on you, French!"

This was not the moment for a too glib answer, so Ray remained silent, waiting. He sensed from Roberts' manner that everything hinged on the next few seconds. He would either have won a desperate gamble—or have lost, irretrievably.

"How was Tony Crossetti the last time you saw him?" the outlaw asked abruptly.

Evart hesitated, almost stammered, "Who?"

Roberts' voice was hard. "I thought you had handled hot ice through Santa Fe. If you know any of the fences there you would have heard of Crossetti!"

"Oh—oh, yes! It's been quite a while—"

Roberts seemed to accept that. He smiled a little, reminiscently. "A good fellow, Tony. And his wife—a real looker, eh?"

Evart shrugged. "If you like Latins."

Suddenly he knew that he had walked into a trap. Sid Roberts was off the table, and one hand slid up quickly to the gap in his coat. His eyes were chill with warning. "I thought as much!" he said quietly. "You've never heard of Tony Crossetti, or you would know he's a woman hater. Never had a wife—can't stand them around . . . Now, how many more lies have you been telling me?"

Ray Evart did not answer. He sat very still, in the position in which Roberts' sudden reach for the gun had caught him.

"I admire your nerve, French—or whatever your name is," Roberts went on, still not raising his voice. There was hardly even anger in his tone, but danger in plenty was there. "I'm more curious than ever to know what brought you up here, and how you knew I was in the rimrock." He stepped to the door suddenly, called without taking an eye off his prisoner: "Nagle!"

For several minutes now men had been riding into the clearing. The mob was gathering, collecting for the big raid on Donover. Through the open door Evart could see them moving in the rain, hard-looking men in ponchos and slickers, carrying rifles and saddles and readying their broncs. Roberts came back to the table.

"I wish I had time to talk to you more now," he said. "But that will have to wait. One of my boys got hurt yesterday and won't be able to go; so I'm leaving him here in camp to keep an eye on you. When I come back from the party tonight we'll pick up where we left off."

Evart said: "I'll be looking forward to it!"

"I bet!"

A man came in through the door. His right arm was in a sling, but the hang of a gun and holster on the other hip showed that he had lost only half of his dangerousness.

"Nagle," Roberts told him pleasantly, "with your wing in that shape I think I'll leave you in camp today. I've got a good job for you here, though." He jerked a thumb at Ray, smiling at him with mockery in his eyes. "I just want you to keep my friend company. And don't let him worry about wearing out his welcome. I wouldn't think of having him leave!"

Nagle exchanged a look with his boss, got his meaning only slowly. Then he began to grin a little, wickedly. "Okay. I'll see that he ain't bored."

"Take over, then. I've got to be going." Roberts shot a last look at Evart. "Better be cooking up a good story for me, when I get back."

He strode out with the same nervous, pent-up energy that showed in everything he did. There was a long silence in the room after that, in which neither of the two remaining made a move. Overhead the rain drummed steadily on the roof, dripped through the holes that opened on dull gray sky. The ravine outside was filled with the shouts of the outlaws, with the pounding and stamping of horses.

Ray Evart had not left his seat. He watched as Nagle slouched away from the door finally, and around the table to the chair Roberts had vacated a while before. He wiped a match to flame on his trousers, touched it to the half-burnt candle; then, as the feeble flame split the darkness of the shanty, he shook out the match and sat down facing his prisoner.

It was then, for the first time, that he recognized Evart. Ray had known him at once, but the other's perceptions appeared to be a little slow. His thoughts showed clearly in his face now, as the mocking look he turned on Ray Evart blanked out and was then replaced, gradually, by a stare of growing hatred.

"Well?" the prisoner said quietly.

Nagle's jaw went hard, his mouth twisting a little. "You!" he spat out. "By God, wait till I—"

He started up, and Ray Evart clenched the chair arms waiting for the call that would bring Sid Roberts back. But that call never came. A new look swept over Nagle's face and he settled back into the chair again, his eyes hard on Evart. At the same time the man's left hand went to his hip and brought out the heavy revolver from its holster. He laid it on the table, close to his elbow.

"No!" he muttered. "Damned if I'll let Roberts in on this. You're my meat, hombre—and after the rest of the boys are gone we'll have our little party without interference."

Ray Evart said drily, "Maybe I should have done more than just wing you last night, when I had a chance to!"

"You can bet you're going to wish you had," Nagle promised. "Legg and me were saddle pards. It was a bad mistake on your part to kill him and leave me alive."

"What are you going to tell Roberts?"

"Oh, I've got that figured out already," the other said promptly. "You tried to get away, see, when my back was turned. There was nothing I could do but plug you—and the bullet went truer than I expected."

"The boss won't like that."

"I'm not worried. He'll be just as pleased to have the job done and over with. You don't think you actually had a chance of leaving Sid's hands alive, do you?"

Ray Evart shrugged. "Oh, I don't know. I've

got lots of chances yet."

They eyed each other. Nagle was a small man, his body a wedge that tapered from bulky shoulders to slim hips and short legs. His head looked small, round, and hard, with a frizz of blond hair and slightly buggish blue eyes. The eyes considered Ray, unwinking, a wealth of hatred behind them.

In a sudden burst of noise, Sid Roberts' crew was riding out. Evart turned to watch the door as they flashed past—a grim outfit, hung with sidearms and with carbines in their saddle scabbards; they rode hunched down into slickers and with heads bent to the driving rain. Ray tried to take a count, and estimated some fifteen riders—all hard and efficient gunslingers or they would not be there with Roberts. It was an army sufficient for any program of deviltry Sid had planned for them.

For a long time the sound of their departure was in the air, dying away to a thread of pulsing rhythm that finally faded. Then the quiet but steady noise of the storm took over in the rain-swept rimrock country.

The space before the open door of the shack now made a muddy soup where many spurred boots and steel-shod hoofs had churned it up. The air already hinted of twilight, though it could hardly have been more than four o'clock.

"Well," Nagle mocked pleasantly, "here we are

alone." He picked up the gun.

"How are we having it?" demanded Evart coldly. "Over with quick, or do you reckon to make me crawl first?"

The man considered. "Well, of course, I've got all afternoon. Wouldn't want the evening to drag, afterwards."

"I see." Evart shrugged. "Good luck to you then. I don't reckon I'll do a very good job of crawling."

"One can always learn," Nagle pointed out, smiling brittly.

Evart said: "Will you answer one question first?"

"I'll listen to it," the man equivocated.

"I'm just curious about the man I was chasing when we hit that cleft in the rim yesterday, and you and your friend charged out at me. He high-tailed it then and I never caught up with him. Did he realize what he was leading me into? Was he one of your gang?"

Nagle shook his head. "He's nobody I know. Probably intended—whoever he was—to bring you into the hills and shake you; but Legg and I just happened to be riding out that way for a look at the Valley, and headed you off. I only caught a glance at him before he was gone into the timber. And we had our hands full with you, by then."

"I take it you didn't want Valley strangers nosing around up here. I can guess why."

"Legg started the shooting," Nagle said. "He was a jumpy sort."

Ray Evart made a small gesture. "Well," he admitted, "you answered my question, all right. Now if we're going to take a little time with this I hope you won't mind if I build myself a smoke?"

"Go ahead. Enjoy it—it will be your last!"

Though he was willing to sit and make conversation with his prisoner, Ray had not an instant's doubt as to his intentions. Nagle was in a killing mood. He had the patience that could wait and taste the savor of a coming pleasure, to put off the fulfillment of it until he had got the last enjoyment from its promise. But there was not a doubt that he would have the deed before he had finished. The death of his friend, Legg, had put a core of hatred into him, and the outlaw's staring blue eyes showed the singleness of his purpose.

Ray Evart considered this as he set his fingers to work with paper and tobacco from the pocket of his shirt. He had an excuse for taking care and pains with the fashioning of his last smoke, so he allowed himself plenty of time—that much more time to think.

The chair he sat in was nearer to the open door than Nagle's, which was also hemmed in by the big deal table. Nagle sat sideward, his left forearm and elbow resting on the table's top, his six-gun lying on the table but riding under the touch of his stubby fingers. The slightest move would put that gun in his hand and the point square on Evart's heart.

Ray thought of all these things. Then he remembered something more that he had detected in Nagle a time or two already. A certain slowness of perception and reaction . . . Could he count on that?

He tapered off the cylinder of rice paper, moistened it, put it to his lips while he weighed the chances. A lot depended on this.

He said: "I don't seem to have a match."

Nagle shrugged, jerked his head at the candle on the table, flickering in the rain-wet breeze through the door. "Use that."

And as the prisoner bent forward Nagle put his left hand on the butt of the gun, ready; but he did not pick it up, because Ray Evart had put himself into an awkward position where no danger seemed likely to come from him.

He was at the edge of the chair, elbows still on the arms of it, his upper body stretched out toward the candle flame. Nagle could not see that he had shifted his weight up onto his spread feet, that Ray's whole body was tensed, ready. Or that his right hand had slipped quietly into the gap where he had left the fourth button of his shirt front unfastened.

The knife came out and flashed forward as Ray hurled it straight at the gunman; with the same motion Evart spun to the side, on the ball of his left foot, and followed the knife with the chair he had been sitting in.

Chapter Eleven

Nagle was quicker than he'd looked. He saw the blade coming and wrenched himself out of its way, and the chair went wide past his shoulder and made the flimsy wall shake behind him as it crashed. At the same time the gun in his good left hand rocked up off the table and thundered; but his movement threw the man off and only the burn of the flame, at such close quarters, seared the Question Mark ramrod's face.

It was all he had hoped for. It would be suicide to tackle a man with a gun out and blazing— even a man with one arm disabled, in a sling. Ray Evart made instead for the open door. He struck the jamb with one shoulder, caromed off and into the rainy twilight.

The other shack stood invitingly near, its door ajar. But he had no reason to think the outlaws had left any of their weapons, and to be trapped in there, unarmed, would be no good. He looked to the left. There was the brush corral, and just this side of it the open-fronted leanto where harness was stored. There were three broncs in the corral—one of them, the gray Ray Evart had ridden up there. And under the flimsy leanto, in a mess of other gear and litter, two or three saddles were lined against the back wall. One might be his own saddle—and his rifle might be in the boot. It was his only chance.

Quickly Ray Evart headed in that direction. Behind him, Nagle had made no outcry; he was the kind who would fight silently, bitterly, doggedly. The sudden crashing of the six-gun told that the outlaw had got his wits about him and was at the door now, shooting after the fugitive.

In trying to swerve away from the bullet Ray slipped in wet mud and went splash, full length. He scrambled up and made the last dozen yards into the protection of the leanto. The gun crashed again, its slug streaking off the rock wall at the back of the open structure. It missed Ray Evart because he was already diving headlong for the narrow protection of the three piled saddles.

He found his own, fumbled at the leathers a moment; after that he sprawled there motionless, panting. The rifle was gone. In dismay Ray Evart speared a quick look around the shadowy leanto, but saw nothing that would serve as a weapon.

And Nagle was coming, on the run. He hauled up a second; the six-shooter bloomed again and Ray ducked as the slug ripped the leather of the saddle, close to his ear. He tried to figure the shots.

That gun should be close to empty by now.

If the man got nearer he would hit Ray. Evart saw that plainly enough. It was almost full dark under the leanto but Nagle apparently had the eyes of a cat. Ray had to keep the man at a distance.

He called out suddenly: "I got my carbine, and I got you lined full in the sights! Throw that gun away if you don't want me to blast you to pieces!"

Nagle hesitated, peering into the tangled shadows while the smoke from the last shot still hung low about him under the beat of the steady rain. The sling on his wounded right arm showed blankly white.

Evart told him again: "Didn't you hear what I said? You make a fine target—and five counts to throw that gun away or I plug you dead center!"

As soon as he said that he slithered back away from the saddle, lest his voice should have given Nagle too good a clue to his position. He had taken the rope down from its horn string, and he had that in his hand now. A rope against a gun . . .

He was counting to himself as he moved, silently. At "two" he was back in the deepest shadows, at the far corner of the leanto. He came to his feet slowly, fingers building a loop in the rope.

In all that time, while the seconds ran on, Nagle had not moved. Ray had him worried. He was debating with himself, undoubtedly, as to whether that threat was truth or bluff; for he would know that Evart's saddle was under that roof, but he couldn't be sure about the rifle.

Suddenly the gun in Nagle's fist began thundering, his lead thudding into the spot where Ray had been. Two shots, and the hammer clicked on an empty; and Nagle, who with his one good hand would make poor time reloading, spun and started running for the protection of the brush corral.

Evart came out of the shadows, his eyes still blinded by the flashing of the gun at close quarters, and cut in behind the running man. The loop spun, shot out toward the man's head and shoulders—fell short. Ray dropped it, sprinted on empty-handed.

Nagle was around behind the corner of the corral now. Nearing, Ray could hear his panting breath as he worked to reload the six-gun. There was the slight click of the gate being closed. The man had a shell or two shoved in and was going to make that do.

Without pausing Evart shouldered around the corner post and closed with him. He saw Nagle's bulging eyes, saw the gun rocking up at him. He clipped out with a hard fist, caught the man's wrist before he could fire and the weapon went spinning into the mud.

Ray plowed in, put a blow against the man's pellet-shaped head that drove him back against the poles. A knee came up aimed at Evart's groin, but he twisted aside and it caught the hard muscles of his thigh instead, sending sharp pain through it.

Then Ray Evart dealt a chopping right, square against the man's jaw, and the fight went out of him. He collapsed, and slid down to a sitting position in the mud with his head falling limply forward.

Ray leaned over him briefly and satisfied himself that Nagle was not hurt badly. The rain that plastered the wiry blond hair down across his forehead should bring him around soon. Ray Evart left him sitting there. It took a minute or two then to locate the gun that had been knocked from the other's hand. He wiped the mud off it, and finished loading it with shells from his own belt.

The leg muscle Nagle had butted with his knee still pained him, so much so that he limped a little from it. Ray flexed the leg as he walked around the side of the corral to where he had dropped his rope.

The gray was well rested by this time. Ray dropped a loop on him and brought his blanket and saddle from the leanto. He looked ruefully at the furrows Nagle's lead had plowed in the good leather; would have traded it for one of the other trees except that his own still looked better to him. He recoiled the lass rope.

As a last precaution he opened the corral gate wide and hazed the two remaining broncs ahead of him and away from the outlaw camp. That would keep Nagle up there, out of the way, when he recovered consciousness—one less of Roberts' men to be contended with.

Ray Evart came in on Squatter Town out of the rainy dark—a soaked, bedraggled figure, his bronc tired from the long downhill job from the high rim. He splashed through Donover River at the ford, and under the dripping cottonwood where he had battled with Tim Riley yesterday afternoon. Topping the bank, he reined in, looking over the settlement. Off to the west, thunder muttered dimly among the peaks.

The huddle of one-room buildings and dugouts was still tonight. Lights showed behind rain-spattered windows. Ray put his bronc forward, found the muddy trail that would take him to Tim Riley's homestead. But when he had reached a bare rise of land that gave a view on the miles ahead, he saw at once that the redhead's place was dark and probably deserted.

He hesitated, wondering what he should do.

What was the name of that girl, now? Then he remembered. He turned the gray and rode back toward Squatter Town; and at the first house he came to he swung down and stepped to knock at the door.

The farmer who opened it stared with suspicion at the figure in the slicker and the cattleman's Stetson. Ray told him brusquely, "I'm looking for the Sothern place. Can you direct me?"

He thought at first the man was not going to answer, but he did say finally: "It's a quarter-mile on up the crick—there's another trail . . . Say, wait a minute," he added, eyes widening, "ain't you—?"

Ray Evart did not wait. He was back in the saddle, leaving the man calling after him, and put his gray off in the direction he had been given. He nearly missed the trail, then got into it and presently raised the lights of another homestead in front of him.

In the night it seemed better cared for than the other squatter places, the house more substantially built. A dog started yapping before Ray was well into the yard, and as he stepped down the animal came in fiercely to smell at his heels, a growl in his throat. The gray swung its head nervously, but Evart ignored the dog and went straight on to the door. The people inside had heard the warn-

ing the dog gave; the door opened before he had
reached it, and Ray stepped into the yellow lamplight it spilled out upon the rain.

An old man, lath-thin, his body bowed from plow
and hoe, stood squinting out at him. Seeing a cattleman, his manner was already hard. "Well?" he
demanded.

Past him Evart saw a door half-opened on another room, and in that room a bed. Its occupant's
face showed as a mere blob of white bandage on
the pillow. It told Evart he had guessed correctly.

"You've got Tim Riley here?" he asked.

The answer was surprising. The old fellow had
a shotgun in the hand that was hidden by the door;
now he stepped back and brought the gun up into
line. "No you don't!" he exclaimed. "You're not
laying hands on him!"

Ray Evart, taken aback by the shotgun, could
only stare at it for a moment; the other, seeing
his advantage, went on in a louder voice, with more
confidence:

"The cattleman's faction wouldn't like nothing
better than to finish the job on Tim, would they—
to come at him now, when he's helpless and unable
to protect himself, and kill him off. You think then
the farmers will buckle down to you—"

Evart had his tongue. "You're reading the signs
all wrong!" he snapped. "I'm here to help you."

"Likely!"

There was bitter scorn and disbelief in that word. Ray Evart stood facing the gun, wondering what he could say to prove his sincerity, and thinking of the precious wasted minutes pounding by. And then the door to Tim Riley's bedroom was opened wide and the girl, Peg Sothern, stood framed in it. The old man's rising voice had brought her from Tim's side, and her tired eyes had a look of alarm in them. "What is it, Pop?" she started to ask, before her look fell on Evart's face and suddenly a newer, harder expression replaced the weariness.

"Ray Evart!" she breathed. She came forward then, put one hand tensely on her father's arm. "It's Ray Evart, Pop—the Question Mark foreman! The one who had the fight with Tim—and the one the sheriff is looking for!"

The old man looked his astonishment; then the shotgun went tighter, in his bony hands. "All right, mister; step inside then if you want it so bad!"

They made way for him, and Ray Evart obeyed because the menace of the gun made anything else impossible. Ducking the low doorway, arms raised, he entered the neat but poverty-stricken room. Peg stepped in behind him, shutting the door against the rain; he stood then with the gun steady on him, water dripping from his slicker onto the clean, scrubbed floor.

"Peg," her father told her, "don't get in the way of the gun. But lift the six-shooter out of his holster. I don't trust any cattleman till his fangs are pulled."

Ray let her take the weapon without protest, knowing that he had no hope of managing quiet and sensible talk with these people as long as any fear of him made them wary; and also hoping that acquiescence on his part would give them confidence in him. He had a chance for a closer look at the girl as she came in and pushed aside the wet slicker, and took Nagle's heavy gun from his holster. She was thin, fined down by the hard work of a shoestring homestead. But she had a good clear look in her large, gray eyes. A pretty girl, if she ever had a chance.

As she stepped away from him, the gun in her work-rough fingers, Ray Evart said quietly: "Now will you let me talk to Riley?"

Old Sothern bristled. "No! You'll save any talking you've got to do, mister, for when the sheriff gets here! I'm sending Peg, now, to find somebody to ride for him."

Evart's jaw went hard. "That's your privilege!" he answered, trying to keep the muffler on that old temper which he could feel now rising within him.

"No doubt you figure that turning me in will put you people in better with the cattle elements—as well as square the accounts for what I did to Tim. Well, all right, send for the law! But meanwhile—let me see him."

"No!"

Desperately, Ray turned to the girl. "I'm appealing to you, miss. I know you hate me for what happened yesterday, and I'm apologizing for that now. But for your sake—not mine—I beg you to let me have just five minutes' talk with Tim Riley —before it's too late!"

His desperate plea must have had a sincerity in it the girl could not miss. She frowned, uncertainty showing in her face; turned to her father. "I guess it can't hurt any, Pop. We got his gun, ain't we? And he took a big chance even coming here; we ought to find out what's on his mind."

The hard old man relented, but only partway. He did not lower the shotgun, and he said warningly: "We better not have any funny stuff. I'll be right behind you, with this greener ready!"

That was all Ray had bargained for. He let the girl precede him into the bedroom—a mere cubbyhole, with an iron bed and a couple of chairs and a lamp on the battered dresser for light. Riley was asleep, his red face looking blunt and firm with the tight bandages covering head and jaw. Sothern stopped in the doorway, suspicion plain in his manner. Peg went over to the bed, leaned to touch the sleeping man's shoulder gently. "Tim," she said. "Tim, wake up! Someone wants to talk to you—"

He groaned and opened his eyes; their expression turned brittle as they fell on Ray Evart standing, in dripping hat and slicker, by the bed. He did not speak.

"I came to you, Riley," the cowman began, "because I know you're a leader in this end of the Valley, and that if I could make you listen to me you would know how to get the rest of them. You're in great danger—all of you—and it may come at any minute!"

The redhead had to talk without moving his broken jaw, letting the words slide out through tight lips. "You mean—the cattlemen?"

"No, no! This is a common enemy, who's worked to set both elements at each other's throats. They struck at both of us, and almost started a war that way. Now they'll wipe us out, singly, if we don't stand to fight together."

Tim Riley studied him, considering these words. Then he said, "Tell me what you know."

Evart gave the three of them a full account of what he had seen and heard in Sid Roberts' rimrock hangout, telling it in the fewest possible

words because of his pressing sense of the time
that had passed since the outlaws started out on
their mission of destruction. "This Duncan," he
told them, "whoever he is, has the stage set for a
large-scale finish. They'll strike both here, and in
the cattlemen's section. But they won't be expecting real resistance."

For a long minute after that, Riley lay looking
at him, his expression not showing whether Ray
had won or lost. Then he said: "What do you think
we should do?"

"I'll leave that to your discretion," Ray Evart
told him, relief pouring through him at his vic-
tory. "You know the situation here; you know
the men you can call on. Naturally, with small,
scattered farms like these it will be hard to fort
up or make a stand. But you must have an idea
what can be done."

Riley said suddenly: "Get me my clothes, somebody!"

He was already sitting up in bed, the covers
thrown partway off. Peg Sothern cried: "No, Tim!
You can't get up! You heard when the doctor—"
The determined look in Riley's eyes silenced her.

From the doorway, old Sothern's harsh voice
said: "I told you something would come of lettin'
this snake of a cattleman talk to him. He's gonna
get Tim outside and finish the job he started."

"Be quiet, both of you!"

In spite of his bandaged jaw, Riley could still make himself heard; and he silenced the pair of them. Ray Evart waited, knowing he could say nothing that would help now.

The redhead added: "Maybe you don't believe what Evart has told us, but I think he's telling the truth. And if he is, then I got no business here in bed. Somebody has to make a defense against Roberts and his crowd when they strike here—and it's going to be me. Now, will you fetch my clothes so I can get out of this?"

Chapter Twelve

It was old Sothern who gave way. He slammed the butt of the shotgun down, hard, and said: "They're in the other room. I'll bring 'em!"

Riley looked at Evart sharply. "How long since you ate, mister?"

"Me?" Ray met his glance in surprise. "Why, I dunno. Not since morning. But there isn't time—"

"Take this man out in the kitchen, Peg," Riley ordered, "and give him some coffee and anything else that's left over from supper. You can't fight a war on a hollow stomach!"

The girl looked as though she were going to bawl. She jerked her head at Ray angrily, and started out of the room; and because the mention of food had really made him conscious of a compelling emptiness inside him, Evart followed her without further argument. At the bedroom door old Sothern stood aside for him, Riley's clothes across his arm. The lean, work-hardened nester gave Evart a sullen look that had bewilderment in it, too. Slower to grasp an emergency than the redhead, and still suspicious of this intruder from the cattlemen's end of the Valley, Peg's father had not yet decided how much he did or did not believe of the tale Evart had brought with him.

The kitchen, like the rest of the house, was small, meagrely furnished, and clean. Coffee simmered in a pot set at the back of the old wood range. Peg Sothern got a cup for Evart, filled it, then without a word set the pot down and went across the room to stand stiffly before the window, her back to him. It was so dark outside that he knew she could see nothing but her own reflection.

Ray Evart held the thick, steaming cup in both hard palms, and looked across it at her back and bowed head. He wanted to say something; all that he could manage was, "I can't blame you for disliking me. But I swear what I've told you is the truth!"

She turned, and there were tears and not anger in her eyes now. "I'm sorry," she said. "I'm actin' something terrible! But Tim's a good man, and— I love him so much! If—if anything happened to him—"

"I know," Ray said. "You're right—he is a good man. I wish you could know how I feel about yesterday afternoon."

She hesitated, her eyes studying his face. "The boys who went for the doc told me what you said about chargin' the bill to you. Of course we ain't goin' to," she added quickly.

"You must," Ray insisted. "It's the least I could do."

She smiled a little, thanking him. "We'll see. Maybe—"

Then as Ray Evart gulped down the coffee, neat, Tim Riley came tramping into the kitchen, shrugging into a waterproof coat. An old Smith and Wesson's was strapped around his waist; Ray Evart's gun had already been returned. Riley had a hat jammed down over the thick bandages that circled his head and jaw, the red hair showing under the edge of it. He said briskly, talking the peculiar way he had to through his set lips: "I'm ready; let's be going."

Outside, the rain was streaking down without a letup, and there was more lightning over the Valley rim. A lantern flickered in the barn where old man Sothern was grimly piling blanket and saddle on a horse for Riley. Ray Evart got his own gray, and stood beside it with the reins in his hands talking to the Irishman.

"There's one question I've asked everyone," he said, "with no answer yet. That stranger, who spied on us and sent me chasing up to the rim yesterday: Who is he? The first sight I had of him was in the door of a dugout, at your settlement at the crossing. Can you tell me anything about him?"

Riley shook his head. "I can't," he said, "and I

should be able to, because I generally keep track of anyone who hangs around there. But I never saw or heard of this one."

"It beats me," said Ray. It seemed now that the stranger did not tie in at any point. He was a separate mystery, entangled in the general knotted web of the Valley's affairs. Ray changed the subject.

"Do you have any ideas yet?" he demanded. "About when Roberts comes?"

The other answered slowly, "I been thinking it over. We can't hope to save all the farms—that's out of the question. Our only chance is to concentrate on one of the bigger places, where there's room to fight, and also where we're pretty sure the raiders will hit. We could surprise them that way, and maybe get in some telling blows."

"A smart idea," Evart agreed.

"I think here at Sothern's is the logical place," Riley continued. "The house is well built, and bigger than others. And it's also one of the first farms they'll come to if they ride in from the north, along the river bank."

Ray said: "What about your own place? It's farther out, isn't it?"

The man hesitated, and his voice as he spoke showed he knew the implications of his answer. "I'll have to let that go. I can't ask the others to leave their own farms unguarded, to help me defend mine. But I think they all like the Sotherns well enough so that they wouldn't object to making the stand here."

"I see," Evart said softly. "So you'll sacrifice your own place, and let Roberts burn it out if he feels like it . . . You're game, Tim Riley!"

The other shrugged, turning away. The lean, hard form of old Sothern came through the rain, the saddled horse trailing and his big dog yelping at his heels. "Here you are, Tim," he grunted shortly. "Go easy getting into that saddle. Here— I'll give you a leg up."

Evart was already mounted. From the back of his horse, as he reined away, Riley told the old man quietly: "Keep that shotgun handy in case Roberts gets here before I'm back. And you better take good care of Peg!"

"That's a damn silly thing to say," the old man snorted, and slapped the pony's rump. "Be off with you!"

The two riders took the trail toward Squatter Town, not saying much until the lights of the first nester house showed near at hand. Then Evart reined closer, and said, "I'll be leaving you now. I can't do any more good here, and there's another angle I want to work on."

Riley did not ask questions. He merely gave a short wave of his hand and said, "All right, cowman. Good luck!" Evart watched as he turned off into the dooryard of the nester house, calling out to the inhabitants. As the door swung open Evart reined his bronc into the muddy trail and touched steel to its flanks.

The wet fields flashed by as the bronc levelled out in the slick trail. Presently it took the dip toward the crossing at Squatter Town, past the half dozen squalid buildings, then under the big cottonwood and, in a splatter, through the shallow waters of the ford. Beyond, Ray Evart left the trail and took the most direct course his bronc could manage in the night, toward the Question Mark.

He found himself listening for the sounds of gunfire, heard instead only the wet slog of his bronc's hoofs, the slither of the rain, and thunder rolling occasionally far off among the peaks. The chief question in his mind was the present whereabouts of Sid Roberts, and his crew. Somewhere in the Valley; but had they already unleashed their attack? And if not, where would the first blow fall?

There was also the matter of the mysterious Duncan. It would help tremendously to know his identity. And one man could be the clue to all these questions—if he could just lay hands on him. Jack Dalley!

He had no good reason to believe that Jack would be at the Question Mark now, but it was the only hunch Ray had and such as it was he would have to play it. He thought he could break Dalley, make him talk; the young man was running in fast company but he was not very tough himself. And tonight Ray Evart was in a mood to employ any kind of desperate measure to get the information he needed.

The rain was thinning out as he approached the Question Mark from the north and west, at an angle that would put the barn between him and the big house and perhaps give him a chance to slip up close without being seen. But there was not much life around the ranch. Lights showed in the house and some of the other buildings, yet Evart had an indefinable sense that the bunkhouse at least was deserted, in spite of the burning lamps. He watched the windows there, could catch so sight of anyone passing behind them.

He got clear to the trees behind the barn unde-tected, and swung down there. The gray's flanks were steaming under the touch of the rain, and Evart gave it a slap with one hard palm. "You've had a rough day, pony," he said. "I'll take a look around and, if I can, get myself a fresh mount. I think you've given me just about all you've got!"

But he did not unsaddle or even loosen the cinches because, after that scene with the sheriff that morning, he did not know what he might run into here and he could have need of the bronc, in a hurry. He left it under the dripping trees, and stepped down toward the blind side of the big barn.

He reached the rain-soaked wall and paused beside it. There were few sounds from the horse pasture, and the corral where the water tanks and hay rack stood was empty. It looked very much as though the Question Mark's crew was riding tonight, and that puzzled Ray and also alarmed him. It meant the ranch would be unprotected in case Roberts struck there.

Was that Dalley's work—part of the plan? It was hard for Ray Evart to imagine a man being that base and disloyal. It did not bode well for Jack, either, if Ray should ever lay his hands on the man again.

He pushed the barn's side door open a crack and listened, hearing only the clomp of a hoof in one of the stalls. Whereupon Ray shouldered on through, giving himself just room enough to clear the door, and closed it again and put his back to it.

Listening like that, in the dark, he heard only a small variety of noises and all of them easy to classify: the rain outside; the stomp and snuffle of the horse eating oats down the aisle; the faint slither of a rat somewhere in the hay. But there was no human sound, and, leaving the door, Ray Evart went quietly down the length of the big building.

As he passed the manger where the horse was feeding it snorted at him. Ray grinned a little, because he thought he knew suddenly what bronc that was. He went on up front to the partitioned tack room. Inside he dug for his matches and thumbed one to life, and shielded the flame while he cast a quick glance around the musty room.

He was nodding to himself as he shook out the light. Very few saddles were stacked in there tonight, and among others Jack Dalley's expensive, silver-rigged affair was missing. That could mean only one thing—Jack was riding. Vain as he was of the saddle that had cost him two months' wages, it would not be out in the rain unless he were using it.

That left Ray Evart exactly where he had been before. Chagrined, he went on back through the barn toward the door by which he had entered; but when he passed the stall where the horse was and it snuffled at him, Ray stopped and considered.

He had thought he knew that bronc; and another match proved he was right. It was the kid Barney's little pet mare. She looked warm and rested, and had a good fill of oats in her. And small as she was, Ray knew the black had good bottom and speed.

"I don't like to borrow you this way without

asking, Molly," Ray told the mare as he reached and got a hand on her halter. "But it can't be helped."

He unfastened the halter and led her up the dark aisle. Molly was not a one man horse, and he didn't expect any trouble with her. Ray took her through the side door, closed it after him, and then went quietly on to the dark trees where the tired gray waited.

He had brought a dry blanket from the barn with him. It did not take long to strip down saddle and gear and transfer them to the back of the little mare. Then he put the halter on the head of the gray and, swinging into the saddle, rode out of the trees with the tired bronc trailing.

What he was going to do now was something he had not planned on. It would take valuable time and also might mean danger for him; but he could not ride off on Dalley's trail and leave whoever might be there at the Question Mark unwarned of Sid Roberts' intentions. This was still his outfit, and Evart still felt a firm sense of loyalty to it.

He moved in toward the rear of the big house, where a light showed in the kitchen. Someone was moving around in there—the cook, undoubtedly. Ray thought he could trust Ben. He brought the horses as close as he dared, left them in a clump of brush and went forward. But in the shadows by the back door he hesitated a moment before showing himself.

Crippled old Ben was not alone. He had company—a woman; they were sitting at the table over the remnants of a late supper, neither eating nor talking much, but with the empty plates and the cold potatoes and a cut of beef forgotten between them. Ben looked worried. Then the woman turned her head a moment and Evart recognized Cherry Bingham.

He had not expected to find her there, but decided she could have come to be with Janet. That was like her, he thought. Without further hesitation he pushed the door open and stepped into the room.

himself.

Chapter Thirteen

They both looked up, startled. Ben came blun-
dering to his feet, while Cherry exclaimed: "Good
gracious!" It was the only thing anyone said at
first.

"Please don't make a fuss," Ray told them.

Cherry said: "It doesn't matter. There's no one
else here."

"Just the two of you? Where are all the rest?"
The woman exchanged glances with Ben. It was
the old cook who answered, "They're out looking
for Miss Craig."

Ray Evart jerked his head up, staring—a tall,
wide figure in muddy clothes, shapeless hat and
wet slicker, gunhandle jutting underneath it. His
eyes were gray and hard. He demanded: "What
are you talking about? Where's Janet Craig?"

"He just told you," Cherry snapped. "She's
gone!" Her voice had the harshness of one who
holds himself sternly in hand. Hearing that note
from big, competent Cherry Bingham was alarm-
ing in itself.

"It happened only an hour or so ago. Jan had
had a pretty hard day—you know, her father;

and the sheriff being here, and all."

"The sheriff?"

"He was looking for you," old Ben put in. He was leaning his crippled body forward over the back of the chair he had just vacated, eyes pinned on Evart, watching the effect of the news on him. "You're wanted by the law now, I suppose you know. Dalley give Joe quite a line, and then he's raving a lot about you pulling down on him."

Ray waved that aside impatiently with the sharp edge of a palm. "I know all that well enough," he said. "About Miss Janet—"

"It was a couple of hours ago, as I said," Cherry went on, with a sour look at Ben for his interruption. "She was all worn out, and I told her to stretch out on the sofa in the front room for a while. Then I went upstairs to do some work and when I came down again she was gone. And nobody saw her leave."

"Is her pony missing?"

"No, still down in the horse pasture. Otherwise I might have thought she had ridden off by herself somewhere—though she didn't say anything about doing that and I'd thought she was too exhausted."

Evart told them bluntly: "I think she was kidnaped."

"So does the sheriff," Ben cackled. "He says you done it."

"Me?"

"Yeah, he's got you booked for every crime in the last five years, including sinkin' the *Maine*. He's after your neck, boy!"

Cherry said, "That's why Ben and I are alone here. All the boys are combing the range for both of you."

"In the dark of night, and raining like sixty," Ben added. "Damned foolishness!"

Ray Evart studied both of them carefully. "Do you think I know where Janet is?"

The pair exchanged looks; it was the cook who answered disgustedly: "Not for a minute. Buckley has some crazy theory that you're holding her until you can get a clean bill of health, or safe passage, or something. It don't make sense to me."

Ray shot a glance at Cherry, saw her corroborating nod. He said, "I'm glad to know where you stand; it'll help me a lot . . ." He added: "Where's Jack Dalley?"

"Dalley? Been gone most of the day," Ben said. "Rode to town with the sheriff and Harry Yates and hasn't been back."

"Then that's where I'll have to head next." With their eyes on him, Evart paced a step away, came back, trying to think straight after the startling information they had just given him. He turned on the cook. "Ben," he asked crisply, "can you still ride—I mean, ride hard?"

The old man drew himself up. "I was a top hand once," he declared. "Nobody says I can't still stick to a saddle. Why?"

"You too," Ray added, including Cherry Bingham. "It's up to the pair of you to help me get warning to the ranchers. I can't make the rounds."

"Warning?" Cherry's look was mystified. "What are you talking about?"

Still standing there, feeling the pressure of wasted moments, Evart told them as much as he could of the situation. "Cherry," he said, "you better get to Sol as quick as you can make it. And Ben, if you can carry the word to the Y Bar, maybe they'll send someone on from there to the other outfits. The trouble is they may not believe what you tell them, if they find out it came from me. But even if they can be halfway prepared, it will help."

Cherry pointed out reasonably: "You don't really think Sid Roberts can attack every ranch in this Valley in a single night, do you? And the nesters, too?"

"Probably not. But he has enough men for two or three effective blows, and the trouble is we have no way of knowing where they may fall. Besides, this man Duncan may have forces at his disposal that we're not counting on. That's why we can't be taking chances."

"Just a minute," Ben broke in. "You've forgotten the Question Mark. What· if they strike
here?"

Evart shook his head. "I haven't forgotten—
but it's something we can't help. With the crew
gone, the three of us certainly couldn't hope to defend it. Maybe one of us can find some of the boys
and send them back."

He was back at the door now, his hand on the
latch. "We've talked too long already. I've got to
be going."

"Where?"

"After Dalley, if I can find him. He's the key to
the whole thing. You two will have to decide for
yourselves what you're going to do."

Ben was whipping off his apron. "I'm riding!"
he declared. "Damned if I'll stand by and let the
buzzards take over this Valley!"

"Saddle a bronc for me while you're at it,"
Cherry Bingham ordered. "If that husband of mine
won't listen to reason I'll beat his ears off. He's
got a prime herd gathered to trail over to the
county seat for shipment next week; it would make
a dandy target for them rimrock thieves!"

"Good for you!" Evart said grimly. "Both of
you. Oh, and, Ben," he added, pausing before he
threw the door wide, "I'm borrowing Barney's

little Molly horse. My gray is out here, pretty well beat out. Would you put him in the barn and put a blanket over him? And throw him down some oats?"

Ben nodded. "Just leave him there. I'll tend to him."

"Speaking of oats," Cherry put in, glancing at Ray shrewdly, "when did you eat last?"

Ray looked at the cold roast without interest, despite his hunger. "I had a cup of coffee at the nesters'," he said. "There isn't time now—"

"There's time to take a sandwich with you. Here!" She sawed off a slab of the meat, slapped bread on it and shoved the food at him. He accepted it, grinning. "Thanks," he said. "You've got a keen eye in you, Cherry!"

Outside, Evart hurried back to his horses. The mare was ready for a run; he stepped up into the saddle and started off at an easy gait, gulping the dry sandwich as he rode. Tired as it was, the gray whickered softly after him.

Ray Evart circled the ranch headquarters, struck the Fowler road and turned into it. Molly started eagerly, but Evart held her down, not wanting to spend her strength too quickly. It was a fraction over six miles to town. He was heading there largely out of desperation, because he had no idea where else in the Valley he might find the man he was after.

The disappearance of Janet Craig weighed heavily on him, dread of the nameless peril that threatened the girl. He could see no way in which that could fit into the pattern that was shaping in Donover this fateful, stormy night. It was part of the muddle of events that included her father's murder—events that could not yet be explained despite the many things that he had learned at Roberts' camp in the rimrock.

The night was vague and formless about him, the general contours of the Valley and its encircling rim lost in the starless dark and the rain. Occasionally a wind came gusting out of the southeast, and each time he listened alertly for the sound of gunfire. Most of the smaller ranches lay in that direction; but there seemed no indication yet that anything was stirring in that section.

And that puzzled him. The time, as nearly as he could judge without the familiar stars to help him, was about eight-thirty or nine o'clock. Sid Roberts must have been in the Valley with his crew for some three hours at least. Then where were they? When would this raid they had set out upon begin? The best answer was that they were holed up somewhere—with Duncan, perhaps?—waiting for an even later hour. Midnight, perhaps—some time when the Valley slept and resistance would be at its lowest ebb.

Ray Evart hoped so. Each hour of self-imposed delay on the part of Roberts would give him that much greater chance to prepare for him.

He reined in sharply. Another gust of wind had brought him something—not gunfire, but the muffled drumming of hoofs on sodden ground. It was gone almost at once, covered by the noises of the night and his own bronc's breathing; hard to tell how many horses he had heard, or from how near or in what direction. He was nearly ready to credit the whole thing to his own highstrung nerves.

After a moment when no other sound came to him he rode on, but more cautiously. A hill breaking before him gave him a dim view, far ahead and below, of the lights of Fowler reflected faintly by the cloud ceiling on the far horizon. The wind was strong against his face now. The storm, which had nearly passed over, was coming back again to the louder voice of distant thunder. Lightning was flickering almost constantly now, like a shutter; and as he came down the hill it suddenly lighted up all the land before him in one intense, eye-punishing glare.

Molly shied, frightened by it. Ray spoke to quiet her, and when the flash dimmed out blinked his own aching eyes hard to get rid of the blindness it left. The darkness now seemed almost a tangible thing, by contrast. But in that brief second Ray had had a good look at the road ahead, dipping to the bottom of the hill through a belt of timber and then flattening out in a straight run toward the town. If anyone was ahead of him on the road, or anywhere in the empty miles of range it threaded, Ray had not been able to see him.

"Don't start hearing things!" he told himself. He urged Molly ahead, and the sensible pony snapped out of its momentary fright and eased away down the slope, in blackness so thick after the lightning that Evart could not begin to see anything. Presently, however, the flickering light showed him the dark trees that stood across the trail, and then he was moving in under them on level ground.

A horse whickered.

The sound was startlingly loud—in his very ear, it seemed—and immediately Ray Evart rammed home the steel. Molly leaped ahead at the sharp pain. But it was too late; horses and men seemed to spring out of the very ground, blocking the trail, closing in on him. Ray cursed his own blindness as he pawed at the slicker, trying to get at the six-gun underneath. He never had a chance to bring it out. He was still fighting the clammy oilskin coat when one of the men leaned across and rammed a hard gun barrel into his side. And then another hand than his jerked the weapon from Ray Evart's holster.

"Take it easy, mister!" a familiar voice ordered sharply. "If you ain't the man we want, we won't hurt you. If you are, it'll do you no good fighting back." To the others he called, "Anybody got a dry match?"

Someone sounded off and kneed his bronc in, bringing it. The flame sputtered, flared up weakly, and the man thrust it forward nearly into Evart's face. By the light of it Harry Yates surveyed his prisoner; satisfaction showed in his black eyes but he did not ease the grip on his naked six-shooter.

"I knew it!" he boasted. "We seen you heading down that slope, when the lightning flared up so big; and I says, 'Boys, that right there's the skunk we're lookin' for or I'm a blinded dogie—even if he is ridin' Barney Stong's black mare!' Ain't that what I said, boys?"

The match had burned down to a blackened twist and the man dropped it, cursing his burnt fingers. In the darkness Ray Evart sat silent, inwardly castigating himself for riding so foolishly into the trap they had laid for him under the trees. It was hard to judge how many men had him now— six or seven, mostly Y Bar riders, according to the faces he had seen in those few seconds of matchlight. And now another man was moving in, shoving his bronc into the circle. The boogery animal caused some little disturbance among its neighbors before the rider could quiet it, and that alone would have told Ray Evart who forked its saddle.

"Well, we got him," Joe Buckley piped excitedly. "Good work, men—and a very lucky accident. Rode right into our hands!" To Evart he said: "Are you going to talk now? Where have you got her?"

"You're a damn fool, Buckley!" said Evart, speaking for the first time, and with chagrin and anger crowding his voice. "Do you actually believe for a minute that I took Janet Craig?"

"Now, don't swear at the law, Evart!" Buckley retorted sharply. He added: "Of course I think you took her. Who'd be more likely, than the man who killed her father?"

"I didn't kill him!"

The sheriff said stiffly, "If I had any doubts on *that* score, Evart—or as to anything else you might be accused of—I lost them a long time ago."

"Yes!" Despite his control, Ray could feel that old hot anger rising strongly. "Because I showed you up! Because I wouldn't let you arrest me, and took your gun off you instead! Anybody can see through you, you cheap, tinhorn politician!"

There was a muffled silence for a second before the sheriff could get command of his voice again;

but then, surprisingly enough, his tone was bland with only a hard edge under the smoothness of it. "I don't reckon, Mr. Evart, that you're going to have much success in disarming the law this time. You seem pretty well surrounded. I think you'll stay that way—and I think eventually you're going to tell us everything we want to know about the whereabouts of this missing girl."

The ground wind was stronger now, sweeping past them and ruffling the wet grass on the slope at their backs, brushing down heavy raindrops from the swaying branches overhead, jerking at hat brims and slicker skirts. In the constant play and flicker of the lightning they could see each other while they talked, there in the hush of the rain.

"Will it do any good," Ray Evart asked, managing to keep his voice calm, "to repeat what I tried to tell you this morning about Sid Roberts being in the country? Will it do any good to say that I've been up at his camp, in the rimrock behind the southern wall—and that I know he's planning to wreck this Valley before the night is over?"

Joe Buckley shook his head. In the same slow, emphatic tone he replied: "It would not—not coming from you. It's fantastic! Who ever heard of Roberts working this end of the state?"

"As for that," said Ray, remembering suddenly and wondering angrily why it had slipped his mind before, "in the pocket of my shirt I have a letter, written by Roberts' own hand, to one of his gang; that will back me up. Here—"

"Quit it!"

Harry Yates' voice rasped loud, and the Y Bar owner's gun came up a little. Ray Evart stopped the hand that he had reached toward the gap in his slicker. After that, very slowly and carefully so that his action could not be misconstrued, he unbuttoned the slicker, opened it wide, and slipped his fingers into the pocket where he had placed Legg's note.

It was empty. He tried the other pocket, found tobacco sack and papers, but no letter. He knew then that he had lost it.

Chapter Fourteen

He could only shrug aside that blow of fortune, and without a word lift his arms again with hands shoulder high. Sheriff Buckley stared at him suspiciously a moment longer. "Well?" he snapped. Then he read the answer rightly, and sniggered a little. "Oh, no letter, eh? You never had any either—just stalling for time. Well, we want no more of that! There's a cell waiting for you in the city jail at Fowler," he went on. "You're staying there until I take you into the county seat tomorrow morning."

Harry Yates suggested, "I know a better way to handle him, Sheriff. And a lot quicker."

Buckley whipped his head around at the Y Bar puncher. He said, "If you're thinking what I think you're thinking—foregt it! You men have helped me a lot, but this is the law's prisoner and the law will punish him. I don't like lynching!"

"Now wait a minute!" Harry's voice had anger in it, and a threat. "Remember there's an election next year, Buckley. You're gonna want some Donover Valley votes about that time; but we won't forget it if you take this skunk away from us now

—after we caught him—and take him out of the Valley for some county seat shyster to set free. It just won't go!"

The lawman didn't answer for a moment, and Ray Evart could almost feel the strength of the man breaking down before that warning. It alarmed him; this was a turn on which he had not counted —a turn against which the integrity of a vote-hungry politician was proving a slim reed.

"Go on, Joe!" he spoke out bitterly. "Make it a hundred percent day. Let everybody who feels like it kick around that star that you're wearing!"

That did the trick. Buckley had some pride left, and those scornful words aroused it. He jerked the reins suddenly, nervously, and his jittery bronc backed away and swung around so that it put him facing that entire knot of riders; and then the blue flickering light showed them the gunmetal in his bony hand.

"I said before, Yates," he remarked crisply, "that the sheriff's office doesn't recognize lynch law in this county. What I said once I stick by; and I'm sorry if you don't like it! Now, just for safety, put your guns back in their holsters—all of you—and lift your hands!"

They obeyed him, more from surprise than anything. The sheriff jerked his head at Ray Evart. "You get around here behind me, mister. We'll leave them and head for town by ourselves!"

Ray touched Molly with the reins, and moved her carefully around to the other side of the sheriff's mount. Harry Yates said, a little sullenly, but with respect in his voice: "That's all right, Sheriff—I take it back. I didn't really think you had the guts to back up what you said. But you better let us ride in with you, because this slippery snake could get away from one man, between here and Fowler—"

A sideward kick of Ray Evart's left leg sent the long-shanked spur hard against the flank of the sheriff's horse. The high-strung animal squealed, bucked crabwise into Yates and the others; and as a yell went up Ray spurred Molly and she lunged ahead. He left confusion behind him, made the trees at the south of the trail before the posse could get their storm-scared broncs straightened out. A shot sent a bullet into the branches overhead, missing him widely. After that Ray Evart was off through the dripping trees and they were coming after him.

He crashed through the narrow belt of timber, broke out upon the cross trail that he added south toward the Y Bar and the Valley's other smaller ranches. He turned into this, and Molly surged forward over the easier going.

His pursuers were not yet out of the timber, but

they soon would be. And once they were well on his tail it would be very hard to lose them. Ray spoke to Molly, asked her for all the speed she could give him. He knew, though, that Harry Yates bred fast horses.

The dark bottomland spurred past. A black streak showed ahead, presently drew nearer. It was the course of one of the many small streams that watered Donover. Flickering lightning showed the brush and cottonwoods lining the stream, and the shallow place where the trail crossed it. Beyond was broken range.

Evart knew what he was going to do then, and as Molly took the easy fording he reined her sharply to the left; she sent the water splashing, slipped on a pebble in the creek's rough bottom. He kept her headed upstream for some fifty feet, then pulled her out into an overhanging cottonwood clump. He was out of the saddle immediately, his boot heels catching hold in the slippery mud of the bank. "Easy! Easy now, girl!" he whispered, working up close to her head and getting a grip on the bridge. Molly's breath whistled strongly as she blew, resting, but he thought the sounds of the storm would cover that. He wanted to be ready to grab her muzzle, though, if she started to whicker when those other broncs came near.

It was a matter of seconds, and then they flashed by him churning up a white commotion in the water, that could be dimly seen. After that silence settled over the crossing as they swept on along the trail to the south.

They would be back, of course; sooner or later they would know that their quarry had eluded them and then someone would think of the brush and trees along the stream. But for the present there was time to breathe, and after that a chance to put distance between himself and that spot before the posse returned.

Ray Evart let the tension run out of him. He slapped the mare affectionately, said, "Good horse, Molly!" And then he froze, with his hand still on the sleek black neck.

Something was there with them, on the muddy bank. He heard again the vague moving of a body, the sudden sound of rasping, labored breath. He started to reach under the tail of his slicker, and remembered again that the six-shooter was gone, as well as the rifle from its saddle boot. Unarmed, he crouched listening; and then, in a flash of the storm, he saw the man.

The stranger lay on his back in the mud, stirring feebly and fighting for wind, the whole upper part of his body drenched with blood that showed black in the fitful glare. The gray sack suit was a ruined mess now, and he had lost his hat. Thinning hair tossed in the gusting rain, over a gray and ashen face now touched with death.

Ray Evart knelt by him quickly. At his touch the man opened staring eyes; the flame of the match Evart brought to life between shielding palms reflected glassily from them. He choked his breath in, gasped: "I know you!"

"You should!" Evart grunted. "You gave me a good chase last evening, and nearly got me killed." He turned a little sick as he saw the mess the bullet had made of this man. It was incredible, the slow drainage of blood he had sustained and still lived. "Who did this to you?" Evart demanded.

The word came out feebly. "Duncan . . ."

Evart caught at the name. It made him say swiftly, urgently: "You can't last much longer, you hear me? But you can still talk a little. You tell me who Duncan is. I want to know—desperately. Tell me, and I promise that I'll get him for you!"

The dying man rolled his head a little in the mud, and Evart had trouble hearing him. "I wanted to—get him myself. Waited ten years. Ten years of prison—because of him. He could have helped me—that night. The station guard only hit me in the leg; I could have made it, if he— But Duncan went on with the money. He left me—"

He began coughing the blood burbling up hor-

ribly to his lips. Evart prodded him urgently:
"Go on! Finish it! They got you, and you went to
prison hating him. Then finally you got out and
traced him here to Donover. What then?"

"I went to old Craig and told him the truth—
gave him a photograph that proved it. I aimed to
ruin Duncan in the Valley, and even the score.
But when someone killed Craig I knew I'd have to
settle it with a bullet, instead. And tonight I saw
him go by in a buckboard. He had a girl with
him—"

"A girl!"

"I got the first shot—missed him. And he finished me. My horse brought me here—"

The voice faded out. Evart seized the man, almost shook him in his frantic eagerness. "But
who—?"

Then he let the limp form go, and got slowly to
his feet, knowing that this man would answer no
more questions.

So Duncan had Janet Craig—had apparently
walked right into the Question Mark house and
taken her out of it, without a sound or a struggle.
It was astounding to think of; and frightening,
because it showed the sinister nature of the enemy
he was fighting.

Ray Evart pondered these things as he moved
back to his horse, away from the body of the man

whose name he did not know. Molly was fighting the reins nervously, boogered by at the smell of blood; or perhaps she already sensed the hated odor of death. Evart spoke to her soothingly, then stepped up into the saddle.

He jerked her head around, put her into the shallow stream and across it. With the stream and its brush and fringe of trees behind him, he struck out across the black range, giving Molly her head. He had not forgotten Roberts and Yates and the posse that might be returning at any moment from their fruitless chase over the southern road.

This was not the way to Fowler. He had changed his mind now about going there; if Jack Dalley were not with Yates and the sheriff, then Evart had a hunch he would not find him in town, either. He would probably be with Duncan, and Sid Roberts, and their crew. And surely an army that size would not have showed itself in Fowler. Gradually, Evart veered north and west until he was nearly doubled back upon the road he had taken away from the Question Mark; then, feeling that he had lost Buckley and the posse and that they would not be expecting him to head back the way he had been riding when they intercepted him, he opened up and cut straight across range for the Craig ranch.

The gusting wind was behind him now, the rain

slanting against his back; and Molly, ready to get back to her warm stall after this cold wet run, lengthened out as she sensed where Ray was going. A quarter of an hour brought him in toward the ranch headquarters.

Lights still showed in the bunkhouse, but the main house looked dark from that side and Evart guessed that old Ben and Cherry had left on their missions. The whole ranch was probably deserted and Ray rode in openly, swinging down from Molly's back under the tamarisks in front of the dark building.

As he went up onto the porch, however, something prompted him to step to the farther railing and lean over, putting his glance along the black side of the house. A window showed light back there, behind drawn shades, and he could see rain streaking against it. It was the window of the study where old Bob had died. Someone was in there—come, perhaps, on the same mission that had called Ray Evart.

That it was not Ben, or Cherry Bingham, he felt very sure.

Moving cautiously, he pushed open the front door and entered the dark hallway. At the very end of it the partly opened door of the study made a section of light on the wall, and there were the furtive sounds of someone moving about, opening drawers, rustling papers. A spur rang.

Ray Evart stepped aside into the living room; moved cautiously through its clutter of heavy furniture to a writing desk at the farther wall, the glass door of a bookcase above the desk shining faintly to guide him. He found the knob, lowered the writing leaf, and reached into one of the pigeonholes. Among papers and envelopes, he found the revolver that was always kept there.

He broke it, checked the loads by touch. Then, with the gun ready, Ray Evart went softly back through the archway and down the dark length of the hall. When he was halfway to the open door of the study the sounds from there ceased, and he hauled up a moment, wondering. Perhaps he had been heard. On the other hand, it might only mean the searcher had found what he was looking for.

Ray Evart went on, more slowly. The door, standing open only a few inches, was at hand now and the light from the room fell dimly over the hard planes of Evart's face. He listened, but heard no sound; and he could see nothing through the narrow crack between door and jamb.

With a quick shove he sent the door wide, and with the same motion stepped clear into the room and to one side of the doorway. He was met by the fierce blast of a six-gun, fired point-blank at short range.

Jack Dalley stood behind the desk, leaning forward on his elbows with a smoking gun in both hands, trained full on the doorway. Papers littered the floor; a drawer which he had pulled out was sitting on top of the desk with its contents scattered. Powdersmoke swirled about his full, dark face.

He had been waiting like that, ready for whoever it was he had heard in the hall. But Evart's quick sidewise step into the room had saved him from the bullet; it smashed into the wall of the corridor behind him, and before Jack Dalley could pull trigger again Ray Evart fired. The window in back of Dalley went out in a smash of glass as his first shot missed; but the second one did not.

It went, in fact, too true. Evart had wanted Jack alive, very badly, but he had had to save himself and Jack was shooting to kill. At Ray's second bullet the man screamed and dropped the gun, his head rocking back to show the blood that covered what was left of his face. He went to his knees, both hands up on the edge of the desk; his head dropped forward against it then and he slid down, leaving a horrible smear on the polished wood.

Ray Evart, leaning with his back against the wall, thought he was going to be sick. Rain-fresh

air from the broken window, that billowed the
torn shade and helped clear the stench of burnt
powder from the room, saved him from that ig-
nominy. But it could not remove the damage that
he had done there.

Both the unknown partner of Duncan, and now
Jack Dalley who was his only other connection
with that mysterious enemy, were dead—the latter
at Ray's own hand. Evart, who had counted so
heavily on making Dalley talk, could hardly accept
the fact of the man's sudden silencing. But the
blunder had been made, and there was no help
for it.

He had only one hope left—the chance that
had brought him back to the Question Mark and
seemed to be corroborated by Dalley's unexpected
presence there in the study. There was something
in that desk. There had to be. Old Bog had tried
to tell him, last night as he was dying; and the
stranger had spoken of "proof" which he had given
Craig.

And Dalley. Duncan had sent him; or perhaps
Jack had come of his own accord, to find that
proof and use it for his own purposes as a blackmail
threat. That seemed even more likely to Evart,
as he thought about it; why would Duncan have
trusted a slippery character like Jack with damning evidence against himself?

But where could that evidence be? Ray Evart stepped gingerly over Dalley's body and looked at the litter spread around the desk. Perhaps Jack had already found what he was looking for, when Ray had given away his presence in the hall. That gave him the distasteful job of turning over the dead man and going through his pockets. Nothing there.

Systematically, then, with the corpse cooling in a bloody mess at his feet, Ray Evart hunted. He went through the crammed contents of the drawer that Jack had pulled out and set on the desk, then through the other two in turn. He consumed valuable time in that search—but he found nothing at all.

His face was grim at the last, as he grew ready to admit failure. It was bitter, and it left him with a blank wall to face and no way to go ahead. He had failed! So much depended on him—and he had failed!

Then, remembering how crammed with papers old Bob had kept his desk, Ray suddenly thought he knew the answer. He squatted over Jack's body, peered back into the dark opening that the drawer left when removed. Back there, jammed at the end of the narrow space, something showed dimly. He reached and got it out, an envelope covered with a solid layer of dust—the one additional item that the already crowded drawer had refused to hold.

It had the name "Duncan" printed on it in ink, if there had been any doubt. As Ray Evart ripped it open, a sheaf of yellowed papers came out in his hand—newspaper clippings, for the most part, dating as far as ten years back; and one faded reward dodger with a photograph. They told much of the career of Tom Duncan—bank robber, rustler, killer, with a fancy figure on his head. The clippings gave no indication that the man had ever been captured or served any sentence for his crimes. The latest one, only five years old, mentioned him in connection with a recent holdup; it speculated on his whereabouts, adding that he had dropped from sight some years before, after a last rich U. P. station job.

Having scanned the news articles briefly, Ray turned again to the photograph on the dodger. Years younger, of course—but plainly recognizable for all of that—it was the strong, handsome face of Will Ormsby.

Chapter Fifteen

The word Jack Dalley brought back from Roberts that afternoon had not set well with the man who called himself Will Ormsby. Sid Roberts, he feared, was getting out of hand.

Sid was not content to carry through the program as Ormsby had planned it. He had seemed jealous from the very start of Will's authority, and suspicious of his Valley partner's intentions. He had gone out of his way to show that no one was running this show for him. Take that matter of the dozen head of Box O steers he had caused to be wantonly and needlessly slaughtered. Ormsby had seen red when Frank Simmons showed them to him, the afternoon before; he had been filled with such a burning rage that he had felt hardly able to maintain control of himself and keep up the part he was playing.

That had been a crude and pointless touch on Roberts' part; the plan was for Ormsby to get old Bob and his foreman, Evart, out of the Valley for a day or two on a stock-buying trip, and leave the field free for Roberts' crew to operate without danger of interference from the strong Question

Mark forces. Roberts had performed on schedule, too, with his double attacks on nesters and ranch men alike that had nearly precipitated a Valley war. But that added touch of slaughtering Ormsby's own stock had been his own idea—needless, uncalled for, malicious.

And now this. Ormsby had planned the finish attack on the nesters of Squatter Town for this evening, to be made by his own crew and the Question Mark riders under Jack Dalley, with the anonymous support of the rimrock gun crowd. The raid could certainly not fail, made with that combined strength; it would wipe out the nester element and place Ormsby in unquestioned position as the cattlemen's leader, with the once-great Question Mark merely backing his initiative. Jack Dalley had been glad to cooperate; a little talk with him over a couple of drinks in town that morning had showed him the whole picture, and his place in it. Jack was bright enough and ambitious enough to see that, with Bob Craig gone, the Question Mark's star was on the decline, and that his own advantage lay in hitching his wagon to a man with ideas like Ormsby.

Foreman of an enlarged Box O, swollen to engulf or dominate not only the Question Mark but eventually every other smaller spread in Donover —that was not a bad mark for a lad of Dalley's talents to hit for. The young man had been so enthusiastic over the prospect that Ormsby had even given him the job of carrying his orders up to Roberts, in the rim country hideout.

And then Roberts had had the audacity to change the program!

Will, putting his light rig and bay mare over the road to the Question Mark, thought these black thoughts and wondered what he could salvage from the ruins. The day-long rain had settled into a miserable drizzle as night closed down, and the cold, wet wind beating at him beneath the flapping side curtains did nothing to help his mood.

It would be fatal, from his standpoint, to pull an all-out raid now. No doubt it would succeed, but it would mean ruin for his own plans. It would mean coming out into the open; shedding his mask as an honest rancher and avowing his connection with the outlaw raiders from the rim. For very definite and vital reasons, Will Ormsby was not ready to do that—yet. But Roberts would not care.

All the outlaw wanted was to get the job over with, get Donover under control, get things organized—so that he could bring his crew down out of that rathole in the rimrock and move in on Fowler, under the political protection of a powerful cattle baron; there, without interference from

the law, he could settle into a civilized existence
with his fine foods and his books and all his peculiar personal tastes, and run Fowler as a private,
wide-open hangout. But Ormsby had his doubts
about that. He was beginning to understand just
how "wide-open" Sid Roberts meant things to be.
He was beginning to wish he had never brought
the outlaw into this, much as he knew he needed
the man's help.

For Sid could not see that for Will Ormsby the
whole problem was complicated by one added fac-
tor—Janet Craig. Because of her, Will could not
move so openly, so bluntly as Roberts. He, too,
wanted the power; but he had to have it in more
subtle ways, that would not revolt the girl and
turn her against him.

Everything was conspiring, it seemed, to force
his hand. The killing of old Bob, for example;
when the old man met him at the front door of
the Question Mark and took him into his study and
confronted him with that startling, damning evidence, there had been no other way to silence
him. Fortunately, he was sure no one had seen
him either before or after the murder; and it had
been no trick to make Janet believe that he had
not arrived until the moment she saw him, some
half hour later. Then, when through incalculable
chance the weight of suspicion began to bear

against Ray Evart, it had begun to seem that he might turn the whole incident to his own advantage.

Now Roberts was adding to his difficulties. Will had the inside edge with the girl, he felt, distraught as she was at her father's death; but he would have to play that advantage for all it was worth. Will Ormsby would have said that he was in love with Janet Craig; whether or not it would have been right to lower that term to cover his feelings toward her, the fact remained that he felt very certain that he would not be satisfied merely to possess the Question Mark. If he could take the girl first, however, then the Question Mark would be his anyway and if he dropped the mask he had worn for her it would be too late for her to change things.

He had reached this stage in his thoughts when he tooled his rig in under the tamarisks and stepped down into the path to the Question Mark's front door. There were lights in the rear and on the second story, but the lower hall and living room were dark in the autumn rain. Will walked lightly through sodden leaves and up the steps to the porch. As a friend of the family, it was a long time since he had knocked before entering the Craig house. Now, finding the door unlocked, he opened it and stepped into the dark hall, stood listening and accustoming his eyes to the poor light. He could hear busy movement in the kitchen, and other sounds from upstairs. He was about to call out when he heard the sofa in the living room stir, as though someone had turned over on it. He moved to the tasseled archway and looked in.

Janet was there, and alone. That pleased him. He took a step into the room, hesitated, and said softly: "Jan."

There was a gasp, then a nervous and sleepy laugh. "Oh—Will!" she answered; and added, "I'm glad you came, Will."

"I hope I didn't disturb you."

"No, no. I was just resting a minute—feel pretty well threshed out. Wait, I'll light a lamp."

"Let me." She was sitting up on the sofa now, relaxed; he could see her dimly as she touched her hair, arranging it. He said, "Or maybe we could sit in the twilight and talk. That's resting."

"Yes," she agreed. "I'd like that." She extended her hand, and in the dark he could sense rather than see the slenderness and the modeling of her round white arm. It sent the pulse to throbbing in his ears. He took the cool fingers and let her draw him down beside her on the deep sofa cushions. "Good, dear Will!" she exclaimed softly, in an access of gratefulness.

He did not release her hand, nor did she withdraw it. There, close to her, with the settling darkness still about them except for the silent noise of the rain, the man who called himself Will Ormsby felt the strong compulsion of his desire, and the confidence of attaining it. He knew suddenly that Sid Roberts, Donover, the Question Mark—all these could go to hell. He wanted this girl, and whatever else happened he could and would have her.

"I thought of you," he said, "as night came on —alone here in this lonely old house. I thought it might help to have someone to talk to."

"And you came all the way from your own ranch—just for that. I do appreciate it, Will. All these past four years—ever since you came to Donover—it seems I could depend on your being there, ready to be called when I needed you!"

"I'm glad you've known that," he said. "I mean, that you could send for me at any time at all. That's more true than ever, now."

They were silent a moment, listening to the rain. Janet stirred then, and said, "Is there any news?"

"News?" He frowned. "How do you mean? About Ray Evart?"

"Yes. That and—other things. I've been alone all day, with no one here but Cherry Bingham. Anything could have been happening outside, and I wouldn't know about it. What of the trouble that started in the Valley three days ago, and the cattle we put across the river onto the farmers' land?"

He considered. "Nothing seems to have come of that. At least I haven't heard of it. Looks to me as if the nesters had taken it lying down—unless they're waiting for more ammunition!"

"That wasn't right," Janet said emphatically. "Even if it was my own dad, I must say that it was wrong for him to violate the farmers' side of the river."

"Well, it's done."

"But it can be undone!" the girl said promptly. "Will, I'm responsible now for every move that the Question Mark makes. It's a little frightening, almost. But it's true and I'm only slowly realizing it. All afternoon I've been thinking about that herd across the river, and I've been waiting for Jack Dalley to show up so I could tell him that it has to be brought back onto our grass—at once."

Will told her: "Too late, tonight. You'll have to wait now for morning."

"Yes, I know. But if Jack won't do it I'll find another foreman who will. Because it has to be, Will! I'm only a girl—but I know something at least of right and wrong; and I know it will be on my head after this if an unjust act by Question

Mark brings war to Donover."

The man was silent for a long moment after that. It was now so dark in the quiet room that they could no longer see each other, even dimly. Will Ormsby said, with a depth of gentleness in his voice: "You are a mighty brave girl, Jan. Anybody would respect those sentiments in you. But it's just for that reason I can't watch you breaking your heart over a thing that's too big for you to buck. I won't let you!"

He could almost feel the puzzlement in the eyes that she turned toward him in the darkness. Janet faltered, and said: "I don't think I know what you mean."

"Is it any secret, Jan?" he persisted more warmly. "Four years now I've been in this Valley, working, building a brand that would be worth something. Four years, and in that time I've seen you nearly every day. And I've watched you mature. You were still an awkward sort of a young person the first time I laid my eyes on you, Jan; very nice, very sweet, but still not much more than a kid. But in four years you've changed under my very eyes—changed into a very beautiful and lovely woman."

"Will!" Her voice had something in it that might have been a touch of alarm; and suddenly she withdrew her hand from his and he could feel the movement as she sat up, a little stiffly. Impulsively he reached for her hand again, touched the cool smoothness of her arm instead.

"Don't act surprised," he begged. "You must have known how I felt. I love you, Jan! I want to marry you. I want always to be near when you need me. Let me help you, Jan—let me take away the burden of trying to manage the Question Mark, all alone!"

He waited, a little breathless, feeling that he had spoken well if a bit heatedly. But there had been no time for an elaborate or cunning preparation. Better, then, to blurt it out like a man with his mind and heart too full for other than the frankest, sincerest confession.

Minutes ran out their length before Janet seemed able to answer; and then she stammered a little. "Will," she said, "I—I really never dreamt you felt that way. Honestly!"

"But how could you have missed it?" he exclaimed. "Why do you think I spent so much of my time at the Question Mark?"

"Well, naturally, you—you were Dad's friend. But as for you and me—after all, we're not quite the same age."

Something chilled inside him, replacing the burning feeling of a moment before. Will Ormsby took his hand off the girl's arm suddenly and stood up.

She was at his side at once, her fingers on his sleeve. "Have I hurt you?" she cried, and added bitterly: "There, you see! I can't even talk seriously without it coming out wrong. You don't want anyone like me, Will," she added, trying to laugh it off but not succeeding. "I'm only a silly girl."

"And I'm an old man!" he finished for her shortly. *An old man!* She thought of him as she had of old Bob, her father! Anger coursed through him, mingling with his passion for her and turning it sour yet, strangely, even sharper.

She had laughed at him—rejected him—because he was old. *Old?* By God, she would find out!

Janet was crying. "I'm cruel!" she exclaimed. "And tactless! I wouldn't have hurt you, Will, for anything. And now you'll hate me!"

He whirled on her. His arms were around her suddenly, his mouth finding hers in the darkness and crushing down fiercely. After the first shock of her surprise she struggled and broke loose, backed away from him with astonished, angry words. Will caught her wrist and jerked her to him sharply.

"You made a mistake," he told her in a low, quick voice, "when you laughed. I came tonight to get you, Jan, and you're going with me. You had your chance to decide whether it was to be by your own consent. I guess you've decided!"

Her astonishment gave way to sudden and intense fear of this man she had thought she knew and didn't. Jan tore wildly at the fingers clamped on her wrist. She cried out: *"Cherry!"*

"Shut up!" Ormsby snapped at her. He added: "She's upstairs. She won't hear you!" Nevertheless he left the girl and stepped quickly to the hallway, listened there a moment. The sound of movement from Janet whirled him back into the room and he caught her at the desk, one hand on the knob to lower the writing leaf. "What are you after?" he snarled.

"Nothing! Let me go!"

He hauled her away, dragged her with him into the corridor and out upon the porch. When she tried to scream he clapped a hand over her mouth.

Full darkness shrouded the space beneath the tamarisks where Ormsby's team and rig stood waiting. He told her sharply: "I can pick you up and carry you out there, and nobody will see me. Or you can promise to go quietly. Which do you want it to be? After all," he added, "I'm not going to hurt you, you know."

Janet Craig had regained control of herself again, though her shock at this astounding change in Will Ormsby was still very great and real. She said in a stifled voice: "I'll go quietly."

Even the cool touch of rain against her forehead could not quite bring home to her that this
was actually happening. It was fantastic, incredible. She let Will help her up onto the seat; then
the springs gave under his weight as he stepped
up beside her and took the reins. *This is not Will
Ormsby!* she thought.

He started the bay mare away at a brisk pace,
and the lights of the Question Mark dropped
away behind them. "Where are we going?" the girl
demanded suddenly.

"To my place," he answered briefly.

The tires of the light rig made a sucking sound
as they skimmed the wet road's surface; the slog-
ging of the bay sounded through, and then the
wind flung a spatter of raindrops in a hard swipe
against the back of the buggy top. Jan shivered.

"I'm sorry!" Will exclaimed. "I forgot to bring
a wrap for you. Here!" He shrugged out of his
coat, and she let him put it around her shoulders.
She settled into the warmth of it; it had a strong
male scent mingled with the sharp tang of Will's
tobacco pouch, in one of its pockets.

He sat beside her, coatless, seemingly unmind-
ful of the chill wet wind or the drizzle that caught
them despite the protection of the buggy top.
Thunder muttered ahead of them; then presently
it was right above their heads, behind the rack of

clouds that warped the sky. Lightning, increasing its fitful chase across the sodden rangeland, gave them a shuttling view of the country about them.

Beyond a stand of tossing trees at the foot of a long hill, they turned into the side trail to the Box O. They had said nothing further, in the twenty minutes that had passed since they had left Janet's home. She demanded now: "What do you think you are going to do with me?"

When he did not answer, she glanced aside at him and saw a frown on his set face. "I haven't thought that far ahead, to tell you the truth," he answered reluctantly. "Frankly, I—hardly expected it to develop this way." He shook his head, smiling a little without any humor behind it. "How far off I was in judging you!"

She said pleadingly: "Did I ever do, or say, anything that might have misled you? I swear I never meant to—"

"No, no!" he answered. "It wasn't that."

"Then why—?"

Will cut her off. "I don't want to talk about it." She felt him fumbling at the coat he had put around her, and then his hand came from its side pocket with pipe and pouch. Wordlessly he set to work cramming weed into the bowl with one broad, firm thumb, putting an almost savage intensity into the simple act. He clamped the pipestem between stubborn jaws, got out a match and scraped it on the frame of the buggy. In the faint light she saw his face, hard and determined, and different from the way that she remembered it.

At the same moment a gunshot clapped ahead of them. Jan caught the flash of it, heard the ripping sound the bullet made as it pierced the heavy cloth of the side curtain. She gasped, cringing away instinctively; and at the same moment Will Ormsby dropped the match in an arc of light that sputtered quickly out.

The horse had shied, pulling the buggy sideways in the road; for the gun had spoken very near to its head. Will cursed the bay. He was off the seat in a crouch, a gun in his hand suddenly and pointed into the rain across the dashboard. A voice cried, *"Duncan!"*

Lightning flared brightly. Jan, staring, saw then such a look of hatred on the face of Will Ormsby as she would never forget. Past his bent figure, with the head thrust forward and the gun silhouetted in his hand, she caught sight of the other man—the one who stood at the edge of the bushes lining a stream just ahead of them. She knew it was that man who had fired the shot; but that was all she could tell, and then the brief moment of light was gone and the blackness swept in again. Ormsby and the other tore it open with the simultaneous crashing of their guns.

The bay reared, neighing its terror. Janet, hands clasped to her ears, crouched back from the horror of the explosions so close beside her. Will fired three times in quick succession; after that she saw him slowly ease down into the seat, the smoking gun still leveled. But there was only a crashing as of a body hitting the brush yonder by the stream, and then silence returning.

Shakily, then, Will slid the gun back into its holster and reached again for the reins. It took a minute to quiet the jittery bay, to get it straightened out so that the buggy could start again on the road to the Box O. They took the dip and splashed across the shallow creek, leaving that moment of gunroar and flame behind them.

Chapter Sixteen

The Box O was smaller and less pretentious than the Question Mark, and the raw newness had not wholly worn off in the four years of its existence. Ormsby's place boasted no touch of beauty such as the tamarisks Craig had placed and trained about the Question Mark house. There were fewer outbuildings and smaller corrals, too.

Will Ormsby, still shaken by the shooting and by the strange echo from his past that had preceded it, came out of his mood with a start as he saw the activity about the Box O tonight. The corrals were full, and despite the rain there was a great deal of movement through the crowded ranch yard. Lights splashed from all the windows. The bunkhouse doors were wide open; men's forms were silhouetted as they passed in and out. The low, five-room ranch house showed life.

Will Ormsby stepped down from the rig before the door, and reached up a hand for Janet. She let him help her down, but took her hand away at once and walked stiffly ahead of him up the muddy path. No word had passed between them since the killing, Will not knowing what to say and she unwilling even to speak to him after the horrible occurrence. When they reached the door and he stepped ahead to hold it open for her, she shrank away a little, instinctively, as the holstered gun at his right hip brushed against her.

She had watched him reload that weapon, methodically, and put it back into its leather pouch. Accustomed as she had been to firearms since childhood, there was something about his deliberate hands as he did that which had put a new aura of horror about him and the gun with which he had killed.

Then they were inside the house. It had one huge room across the front, that opened onto a bedroom, kitchen, and storerooms at the rear. There were makeshift and heavily masculine furnishings—easy chairs, a stone fireplace, and gun racks and a buck's head on the wall. Tonight, the main room seemed full of men. Six or eight of them had a poker game running at a big table at one side, with whiskey bottles and cigarette smoke to help them; they were making too much noise over the game, however, for one to feel that they really enjoyed it or even had their minds on it. Across from them, near the blazing fireplace, Jan saw another man all by himself in the midst of the uproar, reading contentedly. Lamplight shone on the man's strange, mahogany-dark skin, tight across the skull below a receding hairline. He looked up as he turned a page, glanced sharply at the girl and Will Ormsby in the doorway. His eyes had in them a quality that startled her.

They seemed to have no effect on Ormsby. The rancher spoke peevishly. "Made yourself right at home, haven't you, Roberts?" His eyes took in the tall glass at the man's elbow. "Even found the liquor."

"Good stock," Sid Roberts commented pleasantly. "Can't say as much for your library, though." With a look of faint disgust, he put aside the cheap novel he had been reading.

A silence had fallen over the room, as the card players broke their game to stare at the new arrivals. One man who had been sitting with his chair tilted back got to his feet hastily, the cards still in his hand; the chair legs thumped down sharply in the stillness and Janet Craig looked that way. Hope leaped inside of her. "Jack!" she breathed.

Puzzlement showed on Jack Dalley's broad, round face, and he looked quickly from her to Ormsby, under the brim of his scuffed-back hat. Jan cried, half hysterically: "You've got to help me, Jack! Will Ormsby—" She stopped suddenly. Dalley had not moved from his stance against the wall, but something in his frowning look told her suddenly, unexplainably, that he was not there in Ormsby's house by any accident. She knew then that she could expect no help from him.

The thought wilted her as nothing else in the past terrible hour had managed to. In her utter aloneness she felt as though all the strength had run out of her body.

Will Ormsby closed the door, shutting the drip of the rain from the silent room, and stepped past the girl toward Sid Roberts. "I see you brought your whole damn crew here with you," he said sourly. "Don't you care at all what you do to my reputation in this Valley? I've got to keep up some kind of a front, you know!"

Roberts, ignoring that outburst, was looking at the white face of the girl who still stood against the door. He read shrewdly the strained, haunted staring of her eyes. "You forget your manners," he grunted. "Give the lady a chair—she looks about to faint!"

Ormsby stopped in midstride, and turned to follow his glance. He saw at once that Janet had really exhausted her strength, and he went back to her quickly and helped her to one of the heavy leather-bound chairs. She sank into it limply.

"I suppose that's the Craig girl?" Roberts surmised, studying her with interest. "She looks as though she didn't want to come. I thought you were all set with her, Duncan—to hear you tell it."

Will said roughly: "That's my own business. We don't have to discuss it."

A movement from Jack Dalley turned his attention to the latter. Jack had come away from the poker table, and was walking slowly toward them across the bare pine floor. His expression was hard to read, and it was not pretty. "What have you been up to?" he demanded, his tone sounding flat in the stale air. He looked keenly at Janet. "Has he hurt you, Miss Craig?"

She managed a shake of the head.

"You just kidnaped her, then," Jack supplied, swinging his hot glance back to Ormsby. "That's not quite the way I heard it was to happen."

Ormsby shrugged angrily. He knew what was in Dalley's mind. Jack had only come over to his side as quickly as he had because he was sure—as sure as Will himself—that Ormsby held the inside track with Janet Craig. If there had been even a suspicion that Will was not already practically the heir to the Question Mark, it would have taken more persuasion to bring him around. Now he was wondering just what he had let himself in for.

"Take it easy, Jack!" Will said curtly. "You've still got your money on the right horse in this race. Jan just needs a little more time than I had figured, to decide that she wants to marry me."

Jack was still angry, but Will's positive tone had cooled him down considerably. He looked at Janet, dropped his eyes before the accusing glance that she returned. He turned on his heel suddenly, strode to the door and went outside, slamming it after him.

Sid Roberts had watched the whole scene in disapproval. He eyed the closed door, and said: "What about that fellow?"

"Jack?" Ormsby shrugged. "Don't worry about him. He's a little peeved now, but he'll get over it."

The other did not seem wholly convinced of that. He got up from his chair, went to the fireplace and stirred the burning logs with a poker; the wash of the flames showed a thoughtful frown on his mahogany-dark face. Will Ormsby stood behind Janet Craig's chair, watching him above the girl's brown head. Roberts' coolly possessive manner irritated him, the way the outlaw had taken over there as though it were his own house and Ormsby merely a not-too-welcome guest.

The silence of the smoke-fogged room still held, for the poker game waited and the players had eyes only for their chief. They were Roberts men; the regular Box O riders must have been relegated to the bunkhouse while the outlaws took over in the more comfortable ranch house, and

Will did not fail to notice this.

Sid Roberts straightened and put the poker back in its rack. When he turned his glance lit on the men at the table. "You boys better go on outside," he told them. "I want to talk to Duncan."

Without a word they gathered up their cards and chips and tramped out, leaving a mess of stubbed cigarettes and whiskey splotches behind them. They all had interested glances for Janet as they passed her, and she shrank away from them.

The last one left the door open, and Will Ormsby had to step over and close it. It was the final straw. He said, with sharp anger: "Your boys have lived in the woods so long they've forgotten what it's like to be in a house. I wish you'd picked some place else than this to civilize them!"

Sid Roberts ignored him coolly. "About this Dalley," he said, putting his back to the relivened fire. "He acted pretty well huffed. Do you think you'd better keep an eye on him?"

"He doesn't worry me any," Will retorted. "I give him credit for brains enough to know where his bread's buttered."

"I don't think he liked seeing the girl here, though. What if he went to the sheriff?"

"Not Jack—not a chance of it! He's got a much brighter future sticking with us than in letting any loyalty to the Craigs interfere. We're the biggest thing that's ever happened to Dalley, and he knows it."

Sid Roberts was still looking at him with a cold doubt in his eyes that spurred Will's anger. There were many things about the outlaw that irritated him, and now the man's grilling of him on his judgment of Dalley was an added insult.

In a black mood he came away from the door and took the chair Roberts had vacated. But that put him under the directly level gaze of Janet, and the unmasked hatred in her eyes bothered him. He scraped the chair around a little so that he wouldn't have to face her squarely, and looked instead at Roberts, before the fire.

"Well," he said bluntly, dropping the previous subject, "I got your message. You want the big clean-up tonight, eh?"

"Why not?" Roberts wanted to know.

Ormsby shrugged. "No reason—now," he grunted. "The fat's in the fire as far as I'm concerned, anyway." The jerk of his head indicated the silent girl. "I may as well go all the way with you."

Roberts looked at the prisoner. "What happens to her?" he demanded.

"That," Will answered, "is my angle. Don't worry about it." He went on, "How many men have you got?"

"Fifteen—handpicked. And you?"

"A half dozen of my own, and four Dalley brought with him from the Question Mark. With an army like that, we can't miss."

Roberts nodded, satisfied. He got his pipe off the table and fired it up. Will Ormsby, who had lost his own during the excitement of the killing, enviously watched him puff at it and then contented himself with a cigar from the box on the table.

"We'll split our forces," Roberts decided. "There are enough of us to strike in more than one place at once."

The rancher took the cigar from his lips and looked at Roberts sharply. "I dunno," he said drily, remembering. "I dunno whether to let you work out of my sight or not. That's something I've been meaning to bring up with you, Roberts."

Danger glinted in the dark man's eyes. "What?"

"I came back to Donover last night and found some of my own stock, slaughtered. That wasn't part of the bargain. I can tell you it made me sort of angry."

"Oh." Roberts relaxed, and let his look change to amusement. "Just sort of a hint, Duncan—that's all it was. I just wanted you to be sure and remember that my men and I are working *with* you, not *for* you. We're not just hired guns on your payroll. You get out of hand and I'll swat you down!"

Ormsby seemed on the verge of a flare-up at that, but it failed to come off. He sat back slowly, eyeing the spare, spread-legged figure on the hearth rug. Then the cigar went back into his mouth and his jaw clamped tight on it, and a cloud of smoke began building around his head. He said, after a minute, "Your hint cost me good money. Those were prime beefs."

"Don't take it to heart," Roberts said easily. "You'll get plenty back on the investment. As a matter of fact," he went on, "the real reason I had that done was to give you an alibi. If the raid hit you too it would take any suspicion off you."

"Very thoughtful!" Will grumbled sourly. But he said nothing more on the subject.

Roberts went to the window in his nervous, pacing gait, and raised it for a look out at the night. Rain-sound came into the smoky, evil-smelling room, and a welcome gust of fresh cool air. "Leave it open," Will suggested, as the outlaw drew in his head again. "Clear the stench out of here."

"It's going to be a dark night," Sid Roberts observed, coming back to the fire, "with plenty of noise from the storm. That's fine. Surprise is going to be half of it, and this rain will make it twice as easy for us."

"What's your plan?"

"I'll check that one back to you," Roberts answered. "It's your party, and you know the setup. You tell me the program."

Ormsby thought a little as he poured them both drinks from the bottle on the table. He had forgotten much of his anger of a moment before, in his pleasure at Roberts' deference to his judgment. He handed the outlaw his glass, then leaned back and stretched his legs.

"It won't take too large a crew to handle the nesters," he decided. "They're pretty well scattered, and not too numerous at that. They'll put up no organized fight."

"What about that town of theirs?"

Will shook his head. "We just call it that; it's really only a half-dozen shacks and dugouts, that hold a saloon and a few stores where they do their trading. We'll throw some lead in there on our way through, and maybe put the torch to anything that's still dry enough to burn after all this drizzle. For the rest, it's just a matter of picking off the single farms, one by one. I can handle that, with my riders and Dalley's Question Mark men."

"All right." As Roberts turned to set his empty glass on the mantel, his eye fell on the face of

Janet Craig at the edge of the lamplight. He lifted an eyebrow at her, told Ormsby: "The lady's getting an earful, isn't she?"

Ormsby cast his cool, deliberate stare at the girl. "You're beasts," she said. "Both of you." Her voice was so choked with emotion that it barely reached their ears. The words bothered Will, but he drowned the taste of them in another drag at the whiskey.

"I don't think it makes much difference what she hears," he grunted. "She'll know about it anyway, when it's happened, and there isn't much she can do to stop us."

And they went back to their planning as though she were not even in the room.

Sid Roberts said: "While you're cleaning up the west end of the Valley, I'll take my crew against the other ranches. Who needs special attention?"

"Well, there's Yates of the Y Bar. He and the sheriff are off on a wild goose chase, after this Ray Evart who's loose. You can ride right in and set a match to his whole spread, I think, and probably won't even find anyone home to bother you. Harry Yates," he added, "is a loud-mouthed son, but one real blow like that should take all the wind out of him."

The outlaw nodded, a look of satisfaction tightening the thinly-stretched skin across his high cheekbones. "Who else?"

Ormsby hesitated. "I just happened to think," he said, "in connection with the Anchor, which lies just beyond the Y Bar, between there and town. If Sol Bingham hasn't shipped yet, and I don't think he has, then there should be a fair-sized gather waiting for you on his north pasture. Yes, I'm sure of that! He told me the shipment is due at railhead next week, and he was starting it off this Friday. Eight hundred head."

"Sounds interesting."

"It's practically a gift," Will answered, with a shrug. "There'll be at most two or three cowhands riding circle, keeping them quiet in the storm. Your boys will never pick up ten thousand dollars any easier."

Janet Craig could keep silent no longer. "Sol's and Cherry's whole future is bound up in that herd!" she exclaimed. "You'll ruin them!"

"That, my dear," Will answered her calmly, without looking at her, "is the general idea. Of course," he added quickly, "I'll be glad later to lend them the money they need to keep their ranch going. I don't mean to run them clear out of Dono-ver. I want to keep them as neighbors—but on my own terms."

She said nothing more, after that one outburst. And now Roberts announced, in his brusque and nervous manner: "Well, it's as dark now as it's likely to be tonight. I'm ready to ride. What do you say, Duncan?"

"I think I'll wait about ten minutes," Ormsby said. "This young lady and I have got to reach an understanding. Now that she knows in general what the program is, I think just a few words will make her see the light."

With a dry nod, Roberts got his hat and slicker off a chair in the corner. He dragged on the hat, slung the coat across his arm, and paused at the doorway with his hand on the knob, to look back. "Better not be too long starting," he warned. "We want to pull the two jobs almost at once— strike quick and hard, so that nobody has a chance to catch their breath or compare notes and see what's happened."

Will Ormsby waved him out. "I won't be here a minute," he grunted. "Just have a few words to say."

Roberts nodded and went out, closing the door. For a long moment there was only the voice of the rain and wind outside the open window. Will looked at the girl, found her eyes fastened in a fascination of horror on his face. It gave him a strange pleasure that he should so completely command her attention, even though it was hatred that moved her. "Well, Jan," he began quietly.

She said, in a whip-lash of speech: "You killed my father, didn't you?"

It made him hesitate, on the verge of denial. But knowing as much as she did of him, she could hardly be fooled on that score. Will said, "I didn't want to, Jan—sincerely, I didn't. The way he came at me, with what he had learned about my past—well, I think I lost my head. I was sorry, afterward."

"Don't touch me!"

He had been coming toward her, pacing slowly as he talked. She flashed out of the chair, went around it and put the heavy piece of furniture between them. The venom in her eyes as she faced him, bent forward a little, her hands white-knuckled and tight on the back of the chair, stopped him. And then Will Ormsby grew cold and mean. "All right!" he told her levelly, but with a leashed ferocity under his words. "I won't waste time arguing with you. I don't need to. After tonight, Donover Valley and everything in it is going to belong to me—and don't think that I'll allow for any exceptions!"

He strode to the door and threw it open. There was great activity in the rain-soaked yard. Roberts and his men were already nearly saddled and ready for the start, in a confusion of horses and men splashing up the rain-formed puddles. Will saw one of his own men, and yelled to him, "Reese! Come over here!"

Turning back to the girl, he told her: "You'll have a few hours to think things over, but the answer's going to be the same in any case. I want the Question Mark—legally; and I also want you. I know a justice of the peace who will arrange it so that I get both—and after that there's not a thing you will ever be able to say or do that can change it!"

Reese came thumping up the porch steps then. Will told him: "Get Dalley, and Gus, and tell the boys to saddle up. We're riding now."

"Dalley's not here," the man told him, frowning. "He pulled out a quarter of an hour ago. He was quiet and mad-looking, and wouldn't say where he was headed."

Will considered that, not liking it. But he shrugged it aside. "Well, let him go," he grunted. "We've still got the Question Mark men he brought us. They'll ride, even without him."

"OK, boss." Reese started away, but Ormsby called him back. "I don't want you to go tonight, Reese. Get Frank Simmons or some other good man, and load your guns. I want you to stay here, at the ranch, and keep an eye on the girl for me. Maybe one of you watch outside, and the other in here—I don't care. But under no circumstances is she to leave—and as far as I'm concerned you can shoot to kill if anyone makes any attempt to see her. Is that clear?"

He did not know why, in that moment, he should suddenly find himself thinking of Ray Evart.

Chapter Seventeen

Reese was a taciturn individual, and tonight his mouth was a closed trap beneath its wiry, whacked-off brush of a mustache. When the turmoil of departing riders had worn out of the night, and only the drip and mutter of the storm remained, he came slouching into the house without a word for Janet Craig. The girl stood by the fireplace and watched him in silence as he went to the abandoned card table, pushed back one of the straight chairs, and dropped his loose-jointed frame upon it.

He gave the prisoner one careful, scrutinizing glance, but after that he paid her hardly any attention. He seemed more interested in the fact that his position commanded a good view of the open window and of both the front door and the one leading into the darkened kitchen; after ascertaining that he picked up a playing card that had been left behind and began turning it over and over in his fingers, rapping each of its corners upon the table top in turn, in a sharp and monotonous cadence.

The minutes dragged out, under the wind, the drip of the rain, and the continuous tapping of the card in Reese's hands, until Jan suddenly exclaimed: "Do you have to do that?"

Reese stopped and cocked a look at her from under a sandy eyebrow. "No," he admitted drily. "But I like it."

She turned away from his look and started toward the window. His voice followed her quickly. "Don't get any ideas. Frank Simmons is right outside. You try to go through that window and he'll stop you—I ain't guaranteeing how!"

Jan had had no intention of escaping, knowing already that it was hopeless. But his words angered her and she turned away from the window and threw herself into one of the heavy chairs. Behind her, the tapping of the card resumed but stopped presently, and she heard Reese shifting to a new position.

Now that she had time to think, the whole meaning of what she had just lived through swept in upon her crushingly: Will Ormsby's villainy, and his murder of her father. (*Then, she thought suddenly, Ray Evart is innocent, and I'm the only one who can prove it—if I ever have a chance!*). She thought of the treachery of Jack Dalley; and the disaster that was aimed tonight at all of Donover. The Valley would never survive the blows that were being struck at it now. In an hour or two everything that had been would be wiped away, and Will and Roberts would rule unchallenged.

When she thought of what was happening to her friends—to people such as Sol and Cherry Bingham—the sick horror that filled her was so great she all but forgot her own predicament.

There was no clock in the big room, and she could only guess at the time. It seemed to Jan that hours must have dragged out their length since Roberts and Ormsby left, yet she had no way to tell exactly. She turned until she could look at Reese. The man was hunched loosely across the card table now. He had his gun out and was working over it, whistling thinly through his teeth. He seemed to pay her no attention.

The slow dripping from the eaves outside the window seemed to indicate that the storm had stopped for a few minutes, at least. The other man Ormsby had left—Frank Simmons—had spent most of his time until now in the protection of the covered porch; he had seized this chance to make a circuit of the building, and now she could hear his footsteps on the sodden earth as he paced slowly beneath the window. The sounds grew louder, and she saw the top of his head briefly; then he moved on along the wall of the house. The footsteps ceased.

Suddenly they began again; and this time Sim-

mons was running. Janet's breath caught in her
throat. She shot a quick glance at Reese but the
other seemed not to have heard. But then the
sounds faded out as the man got farther away
toward the back of the house; after that there was
only silence. The girl decided it had meant nothing, that she was attaching significance and even
hope to trivial things.

Outside, in the wet shadows at the back of the
Box O ranch house, Ray Evart waited. He did not
know yet what had betrayed him, but something
had—perhaps some noise he had made, or more
likely a movement against the darker wall of the
house. Frank Simmons—he had recognized the
man by the glow from the one lighted window—
must have the eyes of a cat. Now as he drew
nearer Evart's hiding place he slowed down and
was coming forward cautiously, crouched a little,
six-shooter jutting ahead of him.

Ray had his own gun ready. He could have
taken a fairly good shot at the man creeping up
on him, but he did not want to risk that, not
knowing how many might be around the ranch. He
had seen no others, of course, since leaving Molly
on the hillside behind him and working down on
foot toward the silent yard; still, there was that
light shining at the front window, showing that

someone, at least, was inside. Janet Craig, he hoped, without having any way of being sure.

He had known the instant Frank Simmons spotted him, and expected at once to have a cry of warning go up. It was fortunate for him that the guard was a nervy sort of man who would be inclined to investigate an unusual sight or sound without calling for help. His lack of caution would put him at a disadvantage.

As Simmons neared Ray pressed farther back against the wet wall and braced his legs firmly. The man came on, unaware. But at the last moment he must have caught sight of the lurker, for he swerved suddenly away and Ray's arcing gun barrel came down inches short, missing him cleanly.

He stepped in at once, reaching hastily for the gun that he saw rising in the other's hand. Evart's one thought was to avoid a shot that would give warning to anyone else who might be around; he felt cold steel as his fingers closed over the barrel, and then sharp agony bit into the fleshy part of his hand. Frank Simmons grunted and jerked at the gun, trying to tear it loose; but after that Ray Evart made another slash with his own gun barrel and it connected behind the man's ear.

The man's hat went tumbling, and then his body turned rubbery and he fell heavily against the foot of the wall. He kept his grip on the gun,

however, and dragged Ray's arm down with him
before his fingers opened and freed the weapon.
Swiftly Evart slipped his own into holster and
then with right thumb eased back the hammer of
the captured gun, releasing the flesh that had been
caught by its sharp prong as Simmons pulled the
trigger.

Lowering the hammer carefully, then, he tossed
the gun away into the darkness. A quick examination told him that Frank Simmons had received
a solid blow and would be unconscious for some
time; and it was unlikely that any sound of the
brief encounter could have been heard inside the
house. So far, then, so good.

His left hand pained him considerably, and he
thought it was bleeding where the sharp gun hammer had struck. Ray flexed it a moment, as he considered.

A dark window broke the wall surface, very
near his head. He went to it and tried it carefully,
found it unlocked and eased it slowly open. Cautiously, he hauled his body across the sill, then
crouched close to the rough boards of the floor
listening and getting the dusty smell of the place
in his nostrils.

He was familiar with the layout of the Box O's
ranch house. This was one of the two small storerooms at the rear of the house, and the door that

he could see now dimly, across the dark clutter of the room, would lead into the kitchen beyond. Evart came to his feet and took the few steps in his heavy, water-logged riding boots, laid a hand on the knob and turned it softly.

Light streaked into the room as he opened the door a crack. It came, not from the kitchen which was deserted, but through the living room door standing open in the farther wall. It showed him only faintly the big wood range and the shine of pots and pans; and then, beyond that other door, the full bright lampshine of the big room. In the same glance he saw Janet Craig.

She sat bolt upright in a chair by the lamp, staring at him. She had seen the opening of the door in the dark kitchen; now, as he pushed it wider, the girl quickly shook her head at him and glanced meaningfully into a part of the living room that he could not yet see.

Ray hesitated at that. He showed her his hand with two fingers spread open, and saw her shake her head again and raise instead one finger of the hand lying in her lap. The man nodded, understanding. She was telling him that there was one man with her in the room, and one only; Ray could guess that the guard was seated in such a way that he could watch the kitchen doorway and would see the intruder if he stepped farther into the room.

Carefully Ray Evart reached under his slicker, lifted his revolver out of leather and palmed it, preparing himself for a lunge that would carry him across the darkened kitchen and put him, triggering, into the door of the living room. But he never had to make it.

For suddenly Janet Craig had whirled out of her chair and started for the closed front door. A man's voice boomed out: "Hey!" Chair legs scraped and then boot heels thumped solidly. Reese came hurrying into Evart's field of vision; he reached Janet, jerked her away from the door just as she managed to get it open. He glared at her while with the flat of one palm he slapped the door shut again. "I told you not to try that!" he started angrily.

By that time Evart was at the threshold of the room. "Drop your gun, Reese!" he ordered. "Drop it and put up your hands, do you hear?"

The girl's trick had given him the advantage. Now Reese whipped around, with astonishment vivid in his face. But the man had courage. Evart's gun was full on him, and the weapon in his own hand far out of line; yet, in a desperate try, he pulled the gun up and fired once while, with the same motion, he lunged wildly aside.

Of course, the shot was bad; it struck plaster

from the wall several feet from where Ray Evart stood. And for a long second Ray held his hand, not wanting to shoot, remembering the pointless killing of Jack Dalley not an hour before. But Reese was going to fire again, and it was a matter of the girl's safety as well as his own. Ray aimed low, and squeezed trigger deliberately and grimly.

Reese screamed; the sound of it, after the double concussion of the shots, was punishing for the eardrums. He dropped his gun, went to one knee, and then it collapsed under him and he fell forward to lie face down, slapping at the floor with his hands, in agony. Quickly Ray Evart went to him. His bullet had smashed the man's knee.

Face white, Ray got the wounded man in his arms and went to the bedroom, staggering under his weight. Janet Craig had overcome her own horror and she hurried ahead to open the door for him. When Ray laid him on the bed Reese tossed and moaned; there was blood on his mouth under the sandy brush of a mustache, from the lip he was chewing.

"Get that bottle off the table in the other room," Ray ordered the girl. While she went for it he hastily cut away the cloth from over that smashed knee, laying the ugly wound bare. Then Jan was back and he took the bottle from her, put it to the man's lips. "Here!" he said. "Take a good, long drag at this. You'll need it!"

Reese gulped down the fiery whiskey, lay back gasping, and Ray set to work on the injured leg.

There was little he could do, with the tools and the pressure of time that he had to work with. But he cleaned the wound and bound it up with strips from a torn sheet, Janet's quick fingers helping him. The leg would never amount to much again; but at least infection would stay out of it now until the doctor should have a chance to work at it. It would not have to be amputated.

Reese was unconscious before they were through with him. They left him like that, blew out the lamp and went into the living room. Ray Evart could feel the sweat standing out on his own forehead. "I hated to do that," he said gruffly. "I always sort of liked Reese. He was no gunman— just a cowpuncher who hired out to the wrong boss!"

A sudden weariness gripped him. Killing, bloodshed—futile waste of life: It went with greed, and greed was in the saddle in Donover and there would be much, much more of this, all around him, before the night was over. And he and every other man would share in it.

It was Janet's need of him that jerked him out of that bitter mood. He thought he saw her falter, as though in reaction from the horrors she had witnessed, and put out a hand to steady her. And the next moment she was in his arms, her body trembling against him with fatigue and with her sobs.

Ray held her awkwardly. It was the first time that he had ever touched her, and he did it shyly and yet with the sweetness of her tingling strongly within him. He even dared to caress the bright brown head that pressed against his shoulder, in soothing gentleness. "Poor kid," he whispered. "What did they do to you?"

She told him, all in a rush. When she described the scene with Will Ormsby, in the dark front room at the Question Mark, Ray's anger grew to an exquisite agony of hatred. Listening, he knew then that he had not yet had his fill of killing, after all. There was one man whose life he had to take—over a six-gun's sights, or even with his bare hands; it mattered little which.

He said, when she was finished: "You said Ormsby went to Squatter's Town, didn't you?" And his voice had a coldness in it that the girl seemed not to notice.

"We've got to help them!" Janet exclaimed. "And the Binghams, and Harry Yates—"

"Don't worry about them," Ray assured her. "They've already been warned." He explained a little about his own experiences, and the warning he had sent by Cherry and the cook. "It's not going to be quite the picnic Roberts and Ormsby are expecting. They're probably in hot water right at this moment."

She said: "But there must be something we can do—"

"There is." He kicked a chair around, made her sit down in it. "You rest a minute," he ordered. "I'm going to get Molly and find a bronc for you."

There were several horses in the corral. He picked out a gentle one and put on saddle and bridle from the tack room. He considered saddling a fresh one for himself, but Molly was rested and he thought he would rather trust to the little mare than to the unknown qualities of some strange animal; he knew he had a lot of riding yet to do, before the night was up.

Frank Simmons had recovered consciousness and was sitting, a dazed heap, with his back against the dark wall of the house. Ray strode over and the man cringed away from him, one arm coming up in futile defense. "Relax!" Evart told him crisply. "I'm not going to hit you again. I just wanted to tell you your pal Reese is inside with a smashed leg. After I've left I think you better get in there and see what you can do for him."

The man nodded sullenly, one hand touching his battered skull.

"If you get a chance," Ray added, "tell him I didn't mean to cripple him. I'm sorry as hell. The same goes for that clout I had to give you, Frank."

There was puzzlement in Simmons' eyes now, but he still did not say anything. Ray left him and went on to the front of the house, the saddled horses trailing. Janet heard him coming and was out on the steps waiting, the night breeze tugging at her hair and dress.

Ray thought the last of the rain had gone out of the night, and the flying clouds overhead seemed on the verge of breaking up. He hoped so. He was weary to the bone of the dreary storm-sound, and the pelting of the rain. He took off his slicker now, rolled it up and lashed it behind the cantle.

Janet still had the coat Ormsby had given her. Ray said: "Will that keep you warm enough?" and accepted her assurance that it would.

"I want you to ride for Fowler," he told her. "It isn't safe at the Question Mark, or any of the ranches. But anyone in town will look after you until this is over."

She asked: "Where are you going?"

"To Squatter Town."

"Then that's the place I'm headed, Ray."

He shook his head. "You know that's impossible. I've got a job to do, and I can't handle it right if you're there for me to worry about."

She was silent a long moment. "You're going after Will Ormsby?" she said then, slowly.

"Yes." Ray added: "And I want you to be in town, with your friends, where I'll know that you are safe. Besides, if you can find the doctor, he ought to be sent out here to look after that poor devil inside."

"I see." Without more words the girl went obediently to the horse Ray had saddled for her. But as he stepped to help her she turned and moved very close to him, with her face tilted up in the darkness.

"Ray Evart," she told him hesitantly, "I said things last night for which I can never forgive myself. Even if Will Ormsby hadn't told me the truth, I should have guessed it. For I know now that you are good, and fine—"

He said nothing. He could only look down into the lovely face, unable to find any words to answer her. Then he found that words were not necessary.

"Please kiss me," she whispered.

The wonder of that moment was still with him, after they had separated and taken their various trails into the night: she toward Fowler, and he for whatever hell awaited him in distant Squatter Town.

...

Chapter Eighteen

The Y Bar buildings and corrals looked empty
and quiet enough, but as Sid Roberts and his men
rolled into range a rifle started speaking, methodically, from the high black opening of the barn's
hay loft door. Roberts pulled rein, surprised; and
the others broke their charge and came back to
crowd their broncs around his, waiting for orders.
But now that they had hauled in out of range the
man in the barn loft held his fire, husbanding his
ammunition.

"What the hell is this?" someone demanded.
"It looks like they were waiting for us."

Roberts studied the situation thoughtfully.
"Only one gun, though. Whoever is holed up in
there is alone, and he knows it. He started in so
soon because he wants to keep us off as long as he
can." The outlaw brusquely gave his orders. "Fan
out," he said. "Swing around and we'll come in on
the place from all sides at once. And knock out
that guy in the loft."

The rifle began again as they moved forward;
but having been warned of its presence they found
it easy to avoid the flashes, and shooting was poor

in the dark. When they came swarming in on the place, its lone defender proved entirely helpless against them.

Sid Roberts, reining in well beyond the danger area, shouted commands, and four of his men tumbled out of saddles and plunged into the dark barn with their six-guns ready.

It turned into a rat hunt, then. Dick Thomas heard them coming at him through the booming echoes of the big building, but he was already nearly out of his head with the pain of that rifle kicking against his wounded arm. Panic touched him. He had presence of mind enough to know they could only get to him up the ladder that poked through the floor of the loft. Leaving the hay door and the hot-barreled rifle, he crept softly in that direction and got his back braced against one of the rough-timbered supports, his feet planted wide in the loose straw. When a head pushed cautiously through the opening he emptied his six-gun at it, wildly.

The shots rolled out their mingled thunder, and the flash of them gave them a clear look at the bloody, bandaged figure sagging against the beam. Sid Roberts' man, who had been unharmed by any of the bullets, held to the ladder with one hand and with the other quickly punched two shots into the darkness, toward the place where the other had showed himself.

He could not have missed, under the circumstances. He listened as the musty blackness rolled in again, and then with satisfaction heard the result of his shooting—heard Dick Thomas' groan and the loose slumping of his body into the loft's carpeting of straw.

Outside, the rest of the job was being taken care of with the same efficiency. A blaze had already been started at the main house, and the raiders were working at the corrals, breaking them down, turning out the stock that was there. Sid Roberts spurred over as the men who had been sent into the barn came out again. The growing light of the burning buildings etched his dark face as he sat the saddle looking down at them and hearing their report.

"One man left behind," he repeated to himself, as though there were something in all this that he failed to understand. "One man, and a wounded one. He must have been the one the nesters shot, day before yesterday; and Yates left him because he couldn't use him out hunting for that Evart gent." He broke off with a shake of the head. "It doesn't add up. Somehow, the man knew we were coming and was waiting for us. But how could he know?"

Nothing here satisfied him. A suspicion, only half

formed in Roberts' mind, was worrying him now as he went on with the work of destruction. And it rode with him as, followed by his crew, he pounded away finally, leaving Harry Yates' burning house and barn and other buildings to make a bright glow on the breaking clouds behind him.

He was still in a sour mood when he sighted the Anchor herd, three quarters of an hour later. It was bedded down in a shallow sink that broke the grassy surface of the Valley floor, but the day-long rain had left the animals restless and they made a dark, shifting pattern there. That was good; the noise of their stirring would cover the sounds of the riders' approach.

Roberts' crew came upon the depression from its northern side. It was shallow but steep-pitched, and like a funnel in shape; the walls leveling out at the broader, eastern end, while at the west they pinched together to make a narrow way down into the sink. "We go in there," Roberts told the outlaw, Mort, who rode beside him. "If there's shooting and the cattle get stirred up they'll run; and we want them headed the other way, so that we can haze them right on out the eastern end of the Valley. It couldn't be simpler."

They veered west then along the rim of the depression, toward the point where it narrowed down. A restless peace lay over the sink, under the stars and the flying rags of clouds that still skimmed over them. The stirring of the herd, the lowing of a few of the cattle, rose to them as they neared the holding point. Down there in the shifting shadows Roberts though he saw a rider or two circling the herd, trying to keep them quiet. That was to be expected, of course. He only hoped there would not be enough shooting to make the cattle hard to handle when its guard was disposed of.

They took the draw at an easy downward pace, holding their broncs under careful rein as they reached the lower level and the herd showed ahead of them out on the floor of the sink. The riders on circle could be seen now—three of them, taking their job seriously and unaware of the danger closing in on them. Enough starlight had gathered in the broad bottom of the sink to make for clear targets.

Sid Roberts lifted one hand in signal; then they poured out of the throat of the draw, in a sudden clatter of hoofbeats and a rush of hard-driven horses.

The gunfire that lashed back at them came totally unannounced, and caught the close-pressed riders full in its blast. Saddles emptied under the first wild, withering sweep of it. Sid Roberts, with the fierce thunder of the barrage mingling with the yells of his men and the screech of wounded horses, fought his own bronc down out of a frantic pitch. He knew no panic. The hand that palmed his six-shooter, hunting for a target, was steady and perfectly contained.

He saw at once the shape of the trap that he had led his men into—a bunching of rifles behind the shelter of scattered boulders, in such a way that they covered perfectly the crowded mouth of the draw. The men who worked those guns were out to do a thorough job, too; the monstrous thunder they built had the herd behind them on its many feet and rolling eastward in quick panic. That herd had played its part. It had made good bait for the trap.

Cursing in a flat, steady voice, Roberts faced into the storm of lead and set his six-gun bucking. But another horse, plummeting sidewards into his, sent it whirling clear around; before he could get it straightened out Roberts got a brief, wild view of the carnage going on there, of the dreadful toll the ambushed rifles were taking.

That one glance gave him all he needed to know, and he sent the spurs ramming savagely into his frightened horse's flanks. The bronc stumbled, then shot forward under him, leaving the tangle of fallen men and horses behind. Roberts, crouched low as he drove straight into the teeth of the guns, felt the sudden burn of lead somewhere across his shoulders. The bronc swerved suddenly, nearly throwing him, as a rifle lashed out nearly in its face. Sid Roberts saw the man behind the gun, dodging quickly as the shod hoofs went past him. The outlaw snapped a shot at him from the six-gun, knew that he had missed; then he had left the guns behind him and the grassy bottom of the sink rolled away ahead, and he knew that, miraculously, he had ridden out of that death trap with his life.

Out in front of him, the thunder of the stampeded cattle shook the ground. He galloped on in their wake, breathing the dust they put like a faint sheen under the starlight, thinking only of laying distance between him and the death that was behind. There were other guns ahead of him, of course; already other men would be at work turning that rush of the herd, which those who laid the trap had certainly expected. But their hands would be full with that job and Roberts gave them little thought.

He reined in presently, perked his bronc around and sat peering back and listening. The slaughter must be over, for the guns had thinned out to nothing now. There was only the sound of the running herd, and the heavy breathing of the bronc between his legs. Slowly, Roberts forced the tension out of his wiry frame; the hands that set to work feeding new shells from his belt into the smoking six-gun were steady enough.

But the white pitch of fury that seethed through Sid Roberts was a trembling and vibrant thing. It put one name on his lips, and unconsciously he spoke it, over and over again, as though it gave him a strange, sweet pleasure: *"Duncan, Duncan . . ."* As he said it he got the gun reloaded and snapped the gate shut and sat there with it in his hands, feeling the cooling metal with the stroke of his lean, strong fingers.

The growing sound of galloping hooves brought him erect, peering sharply. A rider was coming straight for him from the west, and behind him another, and then straggling in at the rear a third. Roberts knew from their frantic haste who they would be, and at once put his bronc in at an angle to cut off the first of the riders. As he closed in the man shied and snapped up a gun; but then he recognized Roberts and veered to him.

It was Mort. Roberts halted and the man reluctantly did likewise, but the horse kept prancing under his nervous hands. "My God, Sid!" he gasped, nearly sobbing it. "Let's go!"

"Wait!" Roberts told him. "Here's a couple more that got through. That's probably all of them."

The pair were close to panic as they came up. Roberts waved them to the left, and led the way toward the lifting rim of the sink; when they were in under the shadow of it they had to skirt it for a quarter of a mile before finding a place shallow enough to force a way up over the pitch of the crumbling bank. But then they were out of the sink, and safely out of the trap that had closed on them with such stunning force.

The three crowded around their leader. One of them was swearing monotonously, in a voice that shook with terror; Roberts told him curtly: "Shut up!" The man went quiet.

"What in God's name happened?" Mort exclaimed, choking.

"We rode into a trap, that's all!" snapped Roberts. "A perfect, beautiful double-cross!"

He could feel their uncomprehending eyes on him, and the men's stupidity angered him. He said, louder, "Yes, double-cross! Don't expect me to tell you why! All I know is I got taken in—by a cheap crook playing a smooth, deep game. Well, he hasn't heard the last of it!"

Some understanding of what Roberts was talking about had begun to trickle into Mort's fear-stricken brain. He frowned, puzzling on it. "You talking about—Duncan?"

"Of course, you fool! Who else? Who was it sent us after that herd, in the first place?"

Mort shook his head. "It just don't make sense,"

he objected. "I don't get it."

"I don't either—and I don't care much," Roberts said. "All I know is that I'll have Duncan's hide for this!"

Another man said quickly, "But it ain't safe, chief—now! Do you realize there's only four of us left? Four—out of all the crew that started with us! We'd better be thinking of getting our own hides to hell out of this Valley, and no bullet holes in them!"

"We're not going!" Roberts shouted at him, and his voice had a touch of fanatical rage in it. "There's Duncan to settle with, first. Didn't you hear me?"

After that they fell into a sullen and beaten silence. They had never seen this quality in Sid Roberts, and it left them somewhat abashed. He had lost his hat, and now his dark head with its high forehead gleaming faintly in the starlight seemed to shine by an evil, inner light of its own— the light of his consuming rage.

Seeing their submission, he quieted down a little. "That's better," he said. And with one lean arm he swung and pointed north and west, toward the river's arc and Squatter Town. "We're riding there," he told them.

Chapter Nineteen

Someone took a shot at Ray Evart as he tried to cross the ford at the nester settlement. He thought the bullet came from the shadowed doorway of one of the stores, but he could not be sure. Everything was quiet and dark there, under the big cottonwood that overhung the shallow stream. Only the whispering of its branches disturbed the night, after the sound of the shot faded.

He did not contest the crossing; he merely shrugged, and turning out of the trail instead sent Molly upstream along the willow-hung banks. Some distance above Squatter Town he put her into the water and crossed there, thus avoiding entirely whoever might be holed up at the settlement. He figured it was better than arguing.

Besides, the man who had shot at him might not have wanted to argue. Ray was thinking of Polk, in particular—Polk, who had led that one-sided attack on him in town last evening. If that one saw a chance to notch his sights on Evart, it would not be safe to underestimate the temptation it might be for him. Despite Tim Riley's faith in him, Ray knew he had no other friends in Squatter Town, and more than one enemy.

He was glad to find someone on guard at the town, however; it controlled the nesters' southern flank, and it showed they had used sense in distributing their forces.

But not far beyond the river, a ground wind coming against his face hauled him up suddenly, listening, and he knew then that the guard at the town was unneeded. For the raiders were not coming that way: They had already struck, from the other end of the sector, and the direction of the sounds told Ray Evart that the gunfire that he heard now, carried faintly by the night wind, came from Sothern's.

He sent Molly forward at once, and the sounds grew stronger as he neared. There was something else, too—a gleam of brightness at the horizon that quickly strengthened. He knew perfectly well what that meant, and from the smallness and intensity of the blaze he judged that it was a haystack and not any of the buildings which the raiders had managed to start.

Presently Molly cleared a swell that gave him a far view across the black sweep of the night, and he could see the burning stack itself and, lighted up by it, the house and barn. Tiny figures showed, too, moving against them; the whole scene had an unreal and wavering look in the wash of the wind-

whipped flames. And at the same moment the
crackling of the gunfire petered out and then there
was no sound other than the galloping of Molly
and the rushing air beating at his own face.

Ray was puzzled by that, and alarmed by it too,
not being able to tell which side had lost the battle.
Riding on into the strange stillness, he watched
ahead for something to explain it. Soon he could
begin to catch a muddle of voices, and the figures
of the men were easier to distinguish as they grew
before him. And then, at last, he was sweeping
head-on toward them and faces were turned, suspicious and startled, as the horse came galloping in.

He reined in, letting Molly blow, and laid a
flat glance over the scene the wavering fire made.
It was too late to save the stack, and they were
letting it burn; by its light Ray could easily distinguish the lifeless huddles that had once been
men. One sprawled loosely at the corner of the
barn, a saddle gun by it. Others were scattered over
the dark ground.

The redhead, Riley, was just straightening from
one of the bodies as he caught sight of Evart. Ray
reined over to him. "Who is it?" he demanded.

"A cowman, I think," Tim told him shortly.
Then Ray, leaning from the saddle, saw for himself.

"One of Ormsby's riders," he agreed. "And the

others?"

"They were all with Ormsby," Riley answered. "About a dozen of them. They hit us with everything they had, but we were ready for them. You got here too late."

"Did you see Ormsby?" Ray persisted.

Riley nodded. "Plain—by the light of the hay they set burning. I had a good shot at him, but he got away unhurt."

A fierce relief sprang in Ray Evart at that news, and with it the urge to ride. But he waited a moment longer, to ask: "How about your own people? Any of them hit?"

"Not to bother about. We stuck to cover and let the others take the risk."

Looking over his head, Ray saw with more attention now the faces of the nesters and the guns that many of them still carried. He looked for and found the white beard of Sothern; and the girl Peg was there, too, looking very tired but as though her blackest night were now over. As she saw Evart's eye on her she smiled a little, wanly, and yet with gratefulness in her eyes.

"Funny thing," Tim Riley was saying, while the others stood in silence and watched this conversation between their leader and the cattleman from across the river. "The business ended before we quite knew it. Someone started shooting from out there behind Ormsby, and it must have rattled his men; because suddenly they broke and scattered. I have no idea who it was came in to help us, though we saw one of them. He rode right into the firelight and took a shot at Ormsby—and missed him."

"What did he look like?" Ray demanded.

"No one I ever saw before. Dark-faced, and partly bald; didn't have a hat on—"

Alarm touched Ray Evart, then. "You say they all rode off? Which way?"

The man with the bandaged jaw pointed out toward the northwest rim. "That way, generally. At least, Ormsby headed in that direction; and the men who broke up the shooting went after him."

"Thanks!" In his haste Ray prodded Molly on a few yards, but then he brought her back again to Riley. "There's just one thing," he said. "The fight is over now—I mean the one between the two sides of Donover River. Old Bob is gone, and the intolerance and the hatred have to go, too. The Question Mark has a new owner—and I think you people will find Janet Craig a different sort of person to deal with. I just wanted to tell you that!"

With those words he pulled Molly away again. Riley called quickly: "Wait, friend! Where are you heading? Won't you need some help?" But he was out of earshot then. From now on, the road was one he would travel alone, the job one that only he was going to have a chance to finish.

If it was not already too late. The very thought put a baffled anger into him, and made him shove the steel at Molly uncaringly. She answered with a fine burst of speed that put the Sothern place behind him, and the lights there; and then the dark stretch of rough country opened up between him and the high rim trail.

It would be ironical now if Sid Roberts took the job out of his hands. For it was Roberts, of course, that Tim Riley had described to him, and the outlaw had apparently turned against his partner. What had brought that change about he would probably never know, nor did he care too much; what concerned him now was the risk of Roberts getting to Ormsby and finishing him before Ray had his own chance.

He reined in suddenly at the lip of a draw, and down below him a gun spoke again, faint with distance. Another answered; the first repeated, sounding still dimmer and farther away.

Ray Evart shook his head grimly. He had lost. In that confused and broken country ahead of him, and in the gloom of the night's cover, he did not see how he could hope to trail that running fight and get his own gun into it before it had ended. And Molly was tiring, from the long stretch she had made for him that evening.

Doggedly, though, he put her forward down the stony draw. He would not give up, until he knew beyond doubt that it was out of his hands and Roberts had cheated him of Will Ormsby's life. He let the little mare take its own pace, however, for it was senseless to sacrifice Molly for a cause already lost.

Time dragged on as he drove deeper into the breaks. The clouds were gone; over to the east, above the rim at the far end of the Valley, a bright band of radiance told of the near rising of the moon. The night, he judged, was close to half gone now.

The white moon topped the rim, spreading its light in a great wave across the flats and contours of the Valley. It showed the broken range in eerie shadows, but it was little help to Evart in keeping the trail of the riders he was trying to follow. With every moment that passed, at the slow pace he had to take now to spare the tired mare, the trail was growing colder and more futile.

Then a new sound ahead of him, that he had not noticed as it grew at the edge of his hearing, called for attention. As it strengthened he knew what it was—a bronc, being ridden hard. He hauled up, listening. No mistake, the horseman was coming directly toward him. Evart eased his six-gun out

and waited with it ready. And then, through rocks
and brush, the man came toward him and he knew
it was the outlaw, Mort.

The other saw him at the same moment, and
jerked on the reins in sharp surprise. Quickly Ray
told him: "Don't try for a gun, Mort! Hold everything!" Mort saw the flash of gunmetal in his
hand, then, and a second later recognized the man
who held it. The growing light showed the astonishment in his face.

"You!" he exclaimed. "French, what are you
gonna do to me?"

Ray shook his head. "That's not my name. I'm
Ray Evart."

"Evart!" Puzzlement grew deeper in the other.
He added: "I suppose that would explain a number
of things, if I just had the brains to figure it out. I
ain't." He shrugged. "So that was just a line you
handed me when I picked you up in the rimrock
this morning. And you got away from Nagle. Kill
him?"

"No; just tapped him on the chin a time or two.
Where's Roberts, Mort? And Duncan?"

"Dead!" A chill touched Ray as he heard it,
although it was what he had expected. But with the
next breath Mort changed it. "Roberts is, I mean.
That devil of a Duncan! He turned on us when
we weren't looking for it, and he shot Sid and the

two others out of the saddle! Damn!"

"And what did you do?" Ray snapped.

"Hightailed it before he could drop me too, of course!" Mort said frankly. "I told Sid he was crazy to try and settle with Duncan after they wiped us out at the Anchor herd. If he'd taken my advice then we'd be out of the Valley by now." He added: "That's what I want to do next—if you're going to let me!"

"One question," Ray told him, "and you can go for all of me. Where is Ormsby—or Duncan, as you call him—now?"

"Damned if I know, or care!" Mort jerked one thumb vaguely behind him. "Back there somewhere. I didn't stop to ask what his plans were."

"All right." Ray lowered his gun, and stepped Molly out of the path. "I'm through with you, Mort."

The other grunted, "Thanks." He still did not move, however. "But damned if I ain't lost. What the hell's the quickest way out of this place? I want to take it."

"Keep to the south," Ray said. "You'll hit a trail that takes you up the west wall and out." He indicated the notch, showing faintly in the near rim. "That's the best way for you."

Almost at once the man was gone. Ray Evart stayed where he was for a long moment, listening to the frantic haste of his flight. The last of the hoof beats had faded out before he moved; and when he did so the uncertainty had left him. His conversation with the frightened Mort had given him the solution to his problem.

He did not hurry; he did not need to. The white face of the moon rose clear of the eastern rim, and still he took his deliberate course.

Mort had probably been gone from the rim trail a quarter of an hour or more when Ray Evart started up. Molly took its steep pitch easily, and he did not prod her. At the top of the trail, where the moonlight made an intense brightness and deep shadows, he dismounted.

In a clump of juniper back from the trail he stripped the blanket and heavy stock saddle from the pony and picketed her so she could get the grass that grew there. He did not take his saddle gun, but left it in the scabbard; when he went back to the trail his six-shooter was the only weapon he carried and the only one which he would need.

He was suddenly very tired, and yet with a keyed-up excitement in him that made it difficult to relax. He forced that out of him. There was a broad, flat boulder near the trail and he sat down there, and put his fingers to the steadying work of building and shaping a cigarette.

All Donover lay spread out before him now, in a mottling of moon and shadow. Looking down at it, feeling the night wind against his face, Ray Evart found it hard to realize the things that had happened there, in the thirty hours that had passed since he last took this trail down from the rim with old Bob and Ormsby beside him.

Well, he decided, God willing that was over. The rivalries that had split the Valley had outlived their day; and when a new sun rose it would be on a range washed clean.

He thought of Janet Craig, then. Soft, sweet Janet; she had kissed him, that night! Ray shook his head. "Don't put anything in it!" he told himself. "She was all worked up—nearly hysterical with worry. Tomorrow—if you live to see tomorrow—you'll go back down there to the Question Mark and you'll go to work as hard as you can, to help her with that job she's shouldered. But you're never to mention what she did—nor will she. It's not in the cards."

Yet, in spite of his cautioning, he knew somehow that this was not true. There had been more than impulse and gratitude behind her kiss. Time would tell that.

Suddenly, a noise on the trail gave him warning. He stubbed out the cigarette, came smoothly to his feet and stood there, waiting, hands empty and the six-gun riding open in its holster. The bronc plodded nearer up the steep way, and then at last swung into view. Will Ormsby pulled rein at sight of Evart.

The man stared at him, unspeaking. Ray said, "It took you longer than I thought to get out of the breaks, Duncan. But I'd have waited all night if necessary. I'm ready now if you are."

Will looked at him a long time, reading the meaning of his presence there, and the name that he had called him, and the tautness of his body as he stood in the narrow trail. Then Ormsby shrugged, his face unreadable. "I guess I'm ready," he agreed shortly.

Ray watched carefully as the man swung down from the saddle, a little heavily; but Will made no attempt to go for his own gun or to make any trick play. They faced each other then, under the weight of the moonlight, their faces half shadowed by the broad brims of their hats. "So you block the trail to me," Will said. "All along, something's stood between me and what I wanted; and now it's you, Evart."

"It was always me," Ray answered. "I didn't know who I was fighting, but at any step I'd have given my life to stop the man who was trying to make a hell of Donover. I'm still ready to make that bargain!"

Will's handsome mouth smiled crookedly. "And if you win—all the things I tried for are yours without another effort, if you want them. Even the girl, and the Question Mark—"

"That last remark wasn't necessary!" Evart retorted coldly. "You better start shooting, Duncan!"

It was Will who reached for his gun first. He brought it out with a skill and speed that Ray had not expected in him. But a sense of the inevitability of this, and of the issues which its outcome had to settle, lent swiftness to his own arm.

The shots mingled their flame and thunder, in the high air above the Valley's rim. With perfect calmness, Ray felt the bucking of the revolver in his hand, knowing with a quiet surety where the lead would go. Then, as Will cried and stumbled, Ray lowered his gun and watched with less emotion than he had expected to feel. Will had dropped his gun. His hands went up, clutching at his chest where the bullet had struck him. He threw back his head for a moment, showing the handsome face full to the bright moon. Then, abruptly, he collapsed.

Ray Evart straightened. He looked at the still smoking gun in his hand, then shoved it, without reloading, deep into its leather holster. After that he turned and walked back toward the trees, and the whicker of Molly greeted him.